WORTH THE RISK

CAUTION IN LOVE: PART 2

K RODRIGUEZ

DEDICATION

I dedicated Caution in Love to my niece, Jessica.

That book was one of the first times she had ever truly seen herself in a book. She could hear the music, smell the cooking, recognize the conversations, the family dynamics, the love. These characters felt real to her because they felt like home.

That right there is the reason I started writing in the first place. Because I spent so much of my life searching for myself in the books I loved and rarely finding her there.

Years later, I'm honored and proud to take up space within the growing Latiné Romance Community alongside so many incredible authors telling stories that deserve to be seen, heard, and celebrated.

So this dedication is for us.

For the first-, second-, and third-generation Latinés in America. For the ones who grew up between languages, between cultures, between worlds. For the ones still learning that our stories deserve space too.

Here's to being seen.

NOTE TO READERS

Worth the Risk is a continuation of Izzy and Chase's story and is intended to be read after Caution in Love.

Similar to book 1, this romance includes open-door intimate scenes and explicit language. Themes in this story include past infidelity (not between main characters), emotional vulnerability, and family dynamics, including references to alcoholism, verbal abuse from a parent, and childhood neglect.

Please read with care if any of these topics are sensitive for you.

PLAYLIST

1. **Sweet Love** - Myles Smith

2. **Unthinkable -** Alicia Keys

3. **Lose Control** - Teddy Swims

4. **Find Someone Like You -** Snoh Aalegra

5. **Moderación** - JP SAXE & Camilo

6. **The Few Things -** JP SAXE & Charlotte Lawrence

7. **All I Can Take -** Justin Bieber

8. **All I Ask** - Adele

9. **Far Away From Here** - Yaeow

10. **Un Ratito -** Bad Bunny

11. **Who's There To Pick Me Up** - Khalid

12. **Dile Luna -** Karol G & Eddy Lover

13. **You & I** - Victor Ray

14. Say Yes To Heaven - Lana Del Rey

15. Risk it All - Bruno Mars

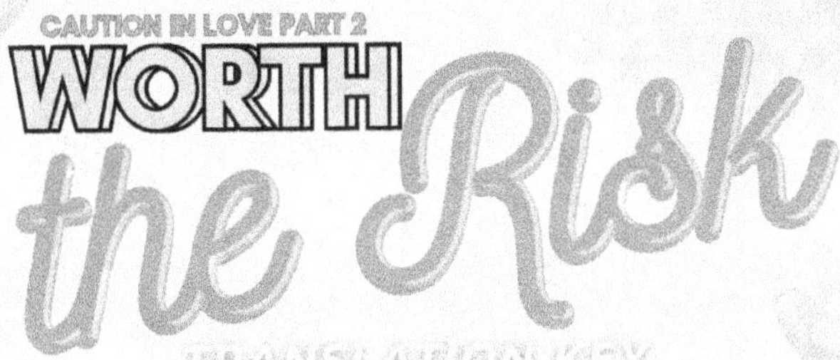

WORTH the Risk

TRANSLATION KEY
(SPANISH TO ENGLISH)

GRINGO – AMERICAN/NON-LATINO PERSON
TÍA – AUNT
AY, MI AMOR – OH, MY LOVE
QUÉ PENA – WHAT A SHAME
PUTA – BITCH/WHORE
NO TIENE VERGÜENZA – HAS NO SHAME
PENDEJO – DUMBASS
AY, MI NINA – OH, MY GIRL
MI COMADRES PRIMA – CLOSE FRIEND'S COUSIN
QUE QUE – WHAT THE WHAT
SE VAN A EXPLOTAR CON ENVEDIA –
THEY ARE GOING TO EXPLODE WITH JEALOUSY
VAMO COMENZAR Y CELEBRAR ESTA NOCHE –
LET'S GET STARTED AND CELEBRATE THIS NIGHT
MI GENTE – MY PEOPLE
POR PRIMERA VEZ – FOR THE FIRST TIME
Y ESTE PAYASO – AND THIS CLOWN
SE ME ANTOJO – I WAS CRAVING IT
PERO YA SE ACABÓ – BUT IT'S OVER
MUEBLES – LIVING ROOM SET/COUCH

K. Rodriguez

♥ REAL CHARACTERS   ♥ BIG FEELINGS   ♥ AND LOVE
THAT HITS HARD

1

CHASE

"*I* love you," she breathes against my lips.

Her words send a thrill down my spine, settling deep in my chest with enough impact to make my whole world shake.

She loves me.

"Are you serious right now?" Izzy's sixteen-year-old sister, Layla, snaps from the hallway, her voice edged with frustration. The sharp click of her heels hits the hardwood as she storms into the bedroom, stopping right beside us.

Izzy and I don't even bother breaking the moment to look her way. The words we just shared hang between us, echoing through me and unraveling everything I thought I knew.

"Can we help you?" she asks, keeping her gaze on mine, her lips curving like she's trying not to smile.

"You two are mad annoying," Layla mutters.

"Mhm. We'll be down in a few minutes," Izzy says, her voice soft, like she's only half paying attention.

Layla groans. "You guys can literally do this whenever you want. Come on already!" She stomps away.

Izzy's mom's wedding is today, and somehow, we're still here in Layla's room—half ready, half not, like the rest of the world can wait.

Layla's retreating steps are barely a blip against the only thing that matters right here, right now—the three words Izzy just dropped. Words I didn't see coming.

"I love you, Isadora."

I lean down, brushing my lips against hers as my fingers slide to the back of her neck, threading into the thick waves of her dark hair as I pull her closer.

The pounding of my heart echoes so intensely; it's in every fiber of my being.

Luck's never been on my side. But those three words falling from those lips, that mouth, this woman, makes me believe that someone up there is finally giving me a chance.

My fingers tighten on the back of her neck, deepening our kiss into a silent plea for her to understand how much she means to me in such a short amount of time.

A soft moan slips out of her as she covers my hand with hers, slowly easing it away as she pulls back. Her heels give her a few extra inches, but even then, as I still tower over her, I tilt my head down. Her face flushes under her make up, eyes darker, lips soft and full, everything about her pulling me in. And with the way she looks at me? With those dark brown eyes shining so bright, I forget how to breathe.

"We're crazy, right?" she asks, her eyebrows rising nervously as she looks up at me. Like we didn't just go and say *I love you* way sooner than we probably should have.

A knot forms in my gut at the sudden doubt in her voice. It's barely been a month. Two, since she crashed into my life and made it feel like something real.

But then I see it—the tiny flicker in her eyes, the way her lips part like she wants to say more. I've seen that look before, the one she gets when she's just about to let me in but pulls back instead. She's scared, but feels this just as much as I do. And hell, maybe I should be afraid, too. But I'm not.

"The craziest, but I was most definitely dropped as a baby. I don't know what your excuse is," I reply, a playful grin dancing on my lips.

"I mean, if getting launched by a treadmill counts, then yeah, that's probably my excuse." She barely gets the words out before bursting into laughter, and I can't help but join her. As our laughter fades, something shifts. Her smile falters, shoulders drop, and her gaze falls to the floor before muttering, "What if we're moving too fast? I mean, we've only been doing this for a month, Chase. What if—"

Hearing her question this—after what we both just confessed— makes my chest tighten. As if time could touch what we have.

I tip her chin up, her eyes meeting mine, then lace my fingers through hers. "Babe, there's no rulebook for this, not when we both know it's real."

Her breath catches as she bites her lip and searches my face. Is she looking for cracks—for the hesitation, the doubt, the one thing that will confirm all the reasons she shouldn't trust this? Trust me?

Because I get it. Her ex didn't just break her trust—he wrecked it. Had her thinking it was real while he was out cheating behind her back. Years she'll never get back. Of course it changed how she sees love.

But I'm not him.

I lift our joined hands, unfolding her fingers and pressing her palm flat against my chest. "And it is real. I feel it. In here." My heartbeat pounds against her palm. "I got you, and you got me, remember? This is real, with or without all the technicalities."

I hold her gaze, hoping in my eyes she can see the depth of what I'm trying to say.

I know Izzy. She overthinks. She guards her heart, convinces herself she's always the one who cares more. And yeah—we might be moving too fast, but I've never been more sure of anything.

Especially when she already feels like forever.

She slowly drags her palms up and down my chest, and just like that, she quiets the noise in my head.

The what-ifs, the tiny doubts, the fear that maybe she sees this as just temporary—they all fade under her touch. She's here. She feels this, just as much as I do.

My pulse kicks up under her fingertips, but I don't move. I let her touch anchor me and let myself sink into the warmth of her hands.

"You're right," she says, and a wave of relief crashes over me. "I do feel it. I've played by the book before, and we all know how that ended. But nothing in my life has ever felt as right as this... as right as you."

She lets out a soft sigh, her eyes fixed on my chest as her finger traces small circles over my dress shirt. "I guess, the unknown still scares the shit out of me a little."

I pull her in, wrapping my arms around her, pressing her close like I can fuse us together if I hold on tight enough. I wish I could make her feel as steady in this as I do—because I'm all in. And if it weren't for the damage her shithead ex left behind, maybe she would be too.

"If this is crazy, then I don't mind losing my mind for you, Izzy," I whisper into her hair.

"Good," she says, her arms tightening around my waist. "Because I don't know how to do this halfway."

Her words wrap around me, sinking in deep. That's exactly how I feel—like I couldn't do this any other way even if I tried.

My grip on her tightens instinctively. My hands slide up her back, over the bare skin her dress leaves exposed–soft, warm, like home.

"Yeah?" My voice is rougher than I expected, like she just knocked the wind out of me.

She nods against my chest, and my shoulders finally drop as I let myself just be here with her.

My lips fall to her temple, her cheek, anywhere I can reach, because fuck, I love her, and now I know she's right there with me.

"Then don't," I murmur against her skin. "We're in this, Izzy. All the way."

Before I can say anything else, a heavy thud echoes from downstairs followed by Layla's sharp voice and Alfonso's manic laugh.

Right. Reality.

And Layla. The last thing I need is her storming back in here again with more complaints about our poor timing—or worse, a full-on intervention about keeping it in our pants before the wedding even starts.

"We should probably get this wedding party on the road," I say, though my hands refuse to let her go.

Izzy sighs dramatically, letting her forehead drop against my chest. "Do we have to?"

I lean back, my hands sliding over her arms—soft and full beneath my palms, my thumbs tracing over the faint lines there. I take in the way she feels before pulling her back just enough to see her face.

"Not much for weddings?" I ask. I've been listening to her huff and puff all morning, but now, up close, I can see it—something deeper sitting just beneath her usual sarcasm.

"I just don't understand why they couldn't go to city hall and sign the damn papers. Why make wedding number three such a big deal?"

"Has your mother ever not made anything a big deal?"

"True story," she says, releasing another heavy sigh before pulling away and turning to grab her purse from the bed. "I'm happy for my mom, but I don't know. I could just do without all this extra fuss."

She pauses in front of the mirror, giving herself one last look. The thin straps cling to her shoulders, soft pink satin hugging every inch of her. That low neckline should definitely come with a warning label. The dress is poured on perfection, pulling in at her waist, gliding over her hips, and that slit flashes the thick curve of her thigh like it's trying to kill me. Every inch of her still wrecks me without even trying, and I'm happily burning every curve into my memory.

She shifts slightly, adjusting the strap at her shoulder, and my pulse stutters. Seeing her like this has me picturing her in white before I can stop myself. A bouquet in her hands, that same fire in her eyes, every vow meant for me. And I can't shake it.

"Is that how you would want to do it?" I can't help myself from asking.

Her brow furrows slightly as she meets my eyes in the reflection of the mirror. "Do what?"

"Your wedding." I try to keep my voice casual, but the second the words are out, my chest tightens. She was with her ex for years. She thought a proposal was coming—and instead, she found he'd been cheating on her. Maybe I shouldn't have brought it up.

Her lips slightly part, then press into a firm line as her eyes avoid mine and she smooths a hand over her dress. "I don't know, Chase." Her voice is careful, almost too light. "I could just do without all of this extra fuss."

I nod, keeping it cool. No big deal. Maybe she just doesn't care about weddings.

Or maybe, just maybe, she stopped letting herself picture one.

"Let's just get this over with," she says, her voice pulling my attention to her as she grabs her purse. She walks past me, the scent of coconut and warm skin trailing behind her.

My fingers twitch, itching to reach for her, to stop her—ask her if it's not too crazy to hope she pictures a future with me. Instead, I stay rooted to my spot, absently rubbing my jaw trying to shake off the sting of her indifference, as she walks out the door.

A second later, she pops back in, leaning against the doorway. "Hey." Her brown eyes meet mine. "I'm really glad I face-planted on that treadmill and landed in your arms." A crooked smile tugs on her lips.

And just like that, doubt loosens its grip on my chest.

Everything else fades as I take her in–the soft curve of her cheek, the way her hair falls over her shoulders, how her skin glows in the light.

"Me too, Izzy. Every single day." I reach for her hand, lacing our fingers together. "Come on, before your sister comes up here and drags us out."

I tug her down the narrow stairway of her childhood home, where yellow walls are overcrowded with family photos in mismatched frames, spanning every year and season of their lives. It's my favorite thing about this place—how every wall, mantle, or crevice where Lulu could hang a nail tells a part of their story.

Halfway down, another heavy thud shakes the floor, and Izzy doesn't waste a second rushing down the rest of the way. Her voice joins Layla's, both of them snapping, "Aiden!"

Aiden, Izzy's six year old nephew, is on the floor in his dress shirt and navy suit pants, laughing his ass off like the stunt was completely worth it. His older brother, Alfonso, cackles from the couch, egging him on, while Layla's got her hands in the air like she's two seconds from committing murder. Lydia, their youngest sister, and Leslie, the oldest and most intense of them all, have been with Lulu all morning helping her get wedding ready, leaving poor Layla down here with these rascals.

"About damn time," Layla shoots back at Izzy. "Not like today's a big deal or anything."

My eyebrows immediately shoot up as Izzy's head jerks back.

Uh-oh.

"First of all, watch your mouth," Izzy warns, instantly raising a scolding finger toward Layla. "And second, you have been late from the moment you were born so don't start rushing others now."

Layla doesn't even look at her. "Oh my God, can we just go? The sooner this day is over, the better," she grumbles instead, standing up and beelining for the door.

I step out of Layla's path before she mows me down. She barely even looks at Izzy, just brushes past like she's already decided she's done with it. I grab the blazer I left hanging on the back of the couch and shrug it on. One thing I've learned from Alfonso, Aiden, and Liam? When it comes to the Peña women, you stay the hell out of their crosshairs.

"Just a minute," Izzy cuts in, blocking her path to the door. "We are not walking out of here with this attitude. Adjust it now. I know today is a lot—I get it. But like it or not, it's happening, and we're going to be there for Mom. Understood?"

Layla huffs, crossing her arms, but the fight drains out of her. "Understood," she mutters, low and sulky.

I glance at my watch, the seconds ticking against us as I picture Center City traffic. We won't be able to avoid it if we don't leave right now. "We really do need to get going or Leslie and Lydia are about to be the whole bridal party."

Izzy straightens her shoulders, stepping to the side. "You heard Thor. Let's go."

Layla mutters, "If you two didn't take so long upstairs, we could've already left."

Izzy flicks her in the ear without missing a beat.

"You are so annoying!" Layla cries out.

I shake my head, biting back a grin. Like Izzy wasn't upstairs just singing the same song a minute ago. But of course, now she pushes it aside to be an example for her little sister and step up for their mom–whether they like it or not.

I'm always in awe of the way they bicker, tease, and test each other's patience, but still, without fail, show up for each other. It wasn't until I met Damon that I understood this kind of security in a person–in a family.

I glance at Izzy, at the way she's wrangling her sister without losing her patience, and it hits me all over again—this is what I want. Not just her, but the life that comes with her.

Mess and all.

2

IZZY

From the doorway, I can't help watching Chase as he heads over to Aiden and Alfonso, who've already returned to their tablets, completely unfazed by the world around them. A bomb could go off, and as long as there was Wi-Fi, these two wouldn't flinch. Dressed in matching muted blue suits and clip-on bow ties, they look like little executives.

Chase ruffles their hair, his massive hands on their little heads, until they both glare at him, their fingers still tapping away at their screens.

"Hey, Sonic and Tails, it's time to go."

"Hold on, I just got to this level!" Alfonso protests.

"Please, Thor!" Aiden chimes in.

"Your aunt said it's time to go. So, that means?"

"Shut it down," they whine, immediately powering off their screens.

He's built this quiet bond with them without even trying, easily folding himself into our lives like he's always been here.

Everyone adores him, even Leslie, and hell, I just told him I loved him.

The words sit heavy in my chest. I don't regret saying them. I just wasn't prepared for them to spill out of my mouth like that. But once they did, there was no taking them back, and absolutely no denying how true they are.

I love him.

Even saying it in my head shocks me and terrifies me all at once.

Not because I don't trust him—but because I know how easy it is to lose myself in something that feels this good.

I'm crazy. No. *We* are crazy.

Chase herds Alfonso and Aiden toward me, the two dragging their feet like I've sentenced them to hard labor instead of a wedding. As I'm about to close the door, I glance around. My stomach dips. "Where's Liam?" I call out, guilt slamming into me for almost forgetting my seven-year-old brother. I push the door back open, and Liam comes flying through the gap, crashing straight into Chase.

"Hey, Knuckles," Chase says, holding Liam up by his arm. Liam shrugs free and pushes past him without a word, climbing into the car like the rest of us don't even exist.

"What was that about?" Chase asks, confused.

I exhale, locking up behind us, and with it goes the urge to correct Liam. He's been quiet all morning, and no matter how much I try to brush it off, I can't shake the tension pressing into my shoulders.

"The move," I reply. Chase's mouth pulls into a tight line before he gives a small nod.

Just last night, at the rehearsal dinner, Mom and Luis dropped the bomb that he's been offered a position at some bigwig hospital in Jersey. Which means right after the honeymoon, they'll be looking for a new place... in Jersey. We all knew them moving in together was imminent, and sure it was sweet of him to wait until after the wedding to officially do it, but now to split the family up and take half of them to Jersey of all places?

Chase's knuckles brush mine as we walk towards the car, his touch gentle and grounding. I instantly curl my fingers around his, holding on tighter than I mean to. He doesn't flinch, doesn't question it, or pull away—just gives my hand the faintest squeeze back.

When we reach Lulu's Tahoe, Chase steps ahead of me, pulls open the driver side door, and to my surprise, scoops me up in his arms. My purse and keys tumble to the street, a startled gasp slipping out of me before it turns into laughter.

"What are you doing, Thor?" I manage between bursts of laughter as he settles me into the driver's seat. He turns around to grab my purse and keys off the ground.

He passes me my things with a shake of his head. "Guess that was a sad attempt at chivalry."

I bite back a grin when I take them from him, my heart melting at his sweet attempt. "Well, you get an A for effort."

The car instantly erupts in exaggerated "awwwws" while Chase jogs around to the passenger side.

"Do you need Thor to buckle you in too, Titi?" Aiden teases from the back, giggling.

"Excuse me, where's my VIP service? I almost broke an ankle climbing in with these heels," Layla chimes in.

Chase presses a kiss to my knuckles before lacing our fingers together. "Sorry," he says. "VIP services reserved."

"Wack," Layla mutters, shaking her head.

I stick my tongue out at her before starting the ignition. The old-school Latin radio station mom keeps the car tuned to blasts through the speakers as I pull onto the road. The second I reach for the dial, ready to switch the station, Layla lets out a blood-curdling scream like I just threatened her firstborn.

"Don't touch it!" she shrieks, practically diving over the center console to crank the volume instead. I flinch, the boys groaning dramatically in the back.

"Lay! What is your problem—" I start, but then the beat settles in, slow and steady, sinking into me like muscle memory as it pulses through the speakers.

In the next second, the whole car is shaking with our shrieks as Layla and I scream the lyrics to "Down" by Rakim y Ken-Y.

A staple from our childhood, thanks to Mom's old-school reggaeton playlist. Of course, this would be the song to pull us from our funk. It played on repeat during every road trip, every Saturday morning cleaning session, or whenever she controlled the aux.

The Spanish parts? We butcher every word but mumble through it without missing a beat. The English chorus, though? We belt out like it's our damn national anthem.

I peek over at Chase just in time to catch the way he exhales sharply, his hand gripping the handlebar above the window like he's bracing for impact. His eyes flicker to mine.

"You are going to be the death of me," he mutters, shaking his head.

I laugh, smiling so wide my cheeks ache—until the rearview mirror catches my eye. In the third row, Liam stares out the window, completely disconnected from everything happening around him. My smile slips away.

I know in Liam's perfect little world, his dad and Lulu would be together. But mom has never given that man the time of day beyond the one night they shared. It's unfortunate for my baby brother, who's far too young to be trying to make sense of it all. But Luis is a good man. Patient, steady, kind, and exactly what Lulu needs. We just need to suck it up and let her have this.

Chase's hand settles on the top of my thigh. He doesn't say a word, but the steady weight of it grounds me. I tighten my grip on the wheel and force my eyes back on the road.

We take the familiar route down the Schuylkill Expressway, weaving through weekend traffic. The closer we get to the city, the more the skyline rises across the horizon—glass buildings catching the midday sun, traffic thickening as we creep closer toward Center City.

By the time we roll into Penn's Landing, it's like the whole city decided to come out for a weekend stroll. People are everywhere —walking, biking, sprawling out along the waterfront like it's already summer.

"Whoa! That's a pirate ship!" Aiden shouts from the back, his forehead pressing against the glass.

"Is that a submarine?" Alfonso adds, eyes wide with excitement. Even Liam leans forward for a better look.

I smile to myself as I ease toward the City Cruises terminal. A line of ships sits docked along the port, their white exteriors gleaming under the bright sun.

Still smiling faintly from the chaos in the backseat, I slide the car into park.

As I unbuckle my seatbelt, everyone else starts piling out of the car–except for Chase. The doors slam one after another, but no one goes far—their voices lingering just outside. Chase's phone buzzes in his hand, and he just stares at it, jaw tight, like he's debating whether or not to answer it. My stomach twists because I already know who it must be.

I'm about to tell him to ignore it when he presses it to his ear and answers instead.

"Hello?" he says into the phone.

I watch him–waiting.

One second... then two.

The lightness in the car vanishes in an instant, the air shifting around us—the storm brewing behind his eyes, locked on the windshield, unmoving.

A single call from her has the power to unravel him and it kills me every single time to see him like this.

I reach for him, my fingers brushing his arm. Just enough to say I'm here.

His grip on the phone tightens, his jaw ticking as he exhales.

"Hello?" he repeats, phone pressed to his ear, eyes fixed straight ahead.

My heart aches at the sight of him like this.

Finally, he lowers the phone to his lap. His hands twitch like he doesn't know what to do with them. Then he taps on the screen, typing into the search bar.

I'm not surprised, but still, my heart cracks right down the middle for him. He hasn't seen his mother since that day in the hospital when she kicked him out of her room— the same night I went looking for him.

"Hey." My voice is soft.

Chase looks at me, and there's a war behind those sharp green eyes.

A long exhale escapes his lips, his chest falling as he moves toward me.

"You good?" I ask, brushing my fingers along the stubble on his jaw.

His eyes fall shut as he leans into my touch.

"I'm better now."

And before I can respond, he leans over, pressing his lips to mine.

It's deep—deliberate—like he's trying to hold on to this moment... to me.

From my side of the car, a chorus of groans erupts behind us, yanking us back to reality and pulling us apart.

"Oh my God, you two," Layla complains.

"Again!" Aiden cries out.

Chase smirks, pulling back as I roll my eyes at the chorus behind us. I push open my door, stepping out into the warm breeze. Chase rounds the car just as I shut the door behind me, his hand finding its place against the curve of my back. Ahead of us, the others are already making their way toward the dock, their chatter mixing with the hum of the city. For just a second longer, Chase and I stand there, the weight of the last few minutes settling between us. Then, without a word, he squeezes my waist.

And we move.

As soon as we approach the dock, Leslie, my older sister, is there, standing impatiently. Her soft, dark curls fall just above honey-toned shoulders, and beside her sits a small white yacht, its name—*Sailin' Love* —etched in bright blue across the side.

"You're late," she says, her voice slicing through the air and her eyes piercing mine. She's dressed in the same soft pink bridesmaid dress, though hers is styled differently with one shoulder bare and the same high slit on the side.

I take a deep breath, bracing myself for her venom.

"Hey, Les." Chase greets her with a kiss on the cheek. She returns the gesture and gives him a small smile before her gaze snaps right back to me.

"We would have been here earlier if these two weren't sucking face every five minutes," Layla quips, brushing past me. I shoot her a dark glare.

"We were not sucking face," Chase adds, clearing his throat. "At least not in front of the boys."

I bite my lip, trying to suppress a laugh. God, this man, this sweet, adorable man.

"They were totally sucking face, Mom," Alfonso says.

"Well, let's keep that"—she points at me and Chase—"to a minimum. Mom wants pictures together before the ceremony."

"Ugh, no!" Everyone but Chase groans.

"Let's just thank God Luis pushed her into getting a wedding planner with her very own team of assistants. Otherwise, it would have been every single one of us, you included Thor, hot-gluing centerpieces throughout the night."

"Stop, you're giving my cramped fingers flashbacks," Layla replies as we all start walking up the dock. I pause at the framed engagement picture of Luis and my mother, sitting on an easel. They look adorable and my mom is practically glowing from happiness.

Watching her in love is one of my favorite versions of her. She deserves every bit of happiness I know today will bring her.

But at the same time, a hint of sadness creeps into my heart. Even though I know it's good, I can't shake the feeling that I'm losing something too. I just got her back, and now —after today —everything changes.

I glance up at the yacht behind her, its pristine deck inviting us aboard. The scent of saltwater fills the air, carried by a brisk breeze that rustles through our hair and clothes.

"They said they'd stay in town," Layla mutters beside me, her voice barely above a whisper.

I reach down and squeeze her hand in mine.

"It won't be so bad, you'll see," I say, keeping the rest of my thoughts to myself.

Layla squeezes my hand back before letting go and stepping onto the gangway.

One by one, we board, stepping onto the lower deck before climbing a short set of stairs leading to the main deck. And when I do—my jaw drops. The space is breathtaking. Tables adorned with sleek, modern decor as they line the perimeter of the deck, each one meticulously set with minimalist center-pieces and sparkling glassware. The soft glow of flickering candles adds an intimate ambiance, and in the center of it all, a small dance floor gleams under subtle lighting.

"Wow," I hear one of the boys let out. I didn't know what to expect when mom mentioned a wedding on the water, but this level of elegance and attention to detail was not it.

We're used to putting ceremonies together on a budget and maxing out her craft store credit cards while she turned into Bridezilla–eventually insisting on doing everything herself. But *Sailin' Love* gleams with polished wood, soft lighting, and elegance that feels like a world away from our usual DIY affairs.

"Good afternoon, everyone," Whitney, the wedding planner, greets us, her tone crisp as she swipes at the tablet locked in her arm. "Your mother is up on the deck with the photographer," she says, flashing a polite smile. I don't miss the way her gaze flicks over to Chase—then down to our linked hands—before quickly nodding toward the curved stairway.

A weight settles in my chest. I glance up at Chase, but if he noticed her glance, he doesn't show it. Stupid doubts try to creep in, but his words from earlier are louder.

He loves me, and dammit, I'm falling harder and harder for him.

Before I can take a step, the yacht rocks beneath us, throwing us off balance and into each other.

"What was that?" Alfonso cries out as I reach out for any solid surface to hold onto. Chase's hand grips my forearm, steadying me.

"Just some choppy waters. There's a storm brewing in the Atlantic, but it's expected to pivot north," Whitney offers. Her tight smile does nothing to reassure us.

"Choppy water, my ass," Leslie mutters, ushering Aiden and Alfonso toward the stairs. "She's been saying that all morning. This is gonna be a shit show."

I reach for Liam's hand as Chase's palm settles on my back, guiding us up the stairs. As soon as we step onto the upper deck, fresh sea air rushes over me, a welcome relief—until I realize the swaying is even worse up here.

Mom stands near a tall railing, her short red hair glowing like fire under the sun. Her ivory gown hugs her frame as the mermaid-style train catches the wind, the photographer clicking away. His dark hair falls into his eyes as he shifts around Mom, chasing the light.

"Mommy!" Liam bolts toward her, and the photographer doesn't miss a beat, capturing the moment as she pulls him into a hug.

A soft smile tugs at my lips. Then—

"Where did Ma find him?" Layla mutters beside me.

I tug on the end of her curls. "Nowhere you need to be looking, jailbait."

The photographer lowers his camera for a second as Layla walks past. I shoot him a pointed glare that makes him quickly refocus on his lens.

"Ma, you look amazing," I say as I reach her.

"Excuse me, when am I anything less?" she quips, arms open.

Layla shoves herself in between us. "What she means is you look beyond amazing. Like, Luis might need one of his doctor friends to resuscitate him when he sees you."

I roll my eyes and move her out of the way. "She was hugging me first."

Mom laughs, pulling me into her arms, the scent of her familiar Dior perfume wrapping around me. The moment she squeezes me, a sudden reel of hugs just like these flashes through my mind, and I'm overtaken by a rush of emotions. She attempts to pull back but I hold on to her tighter. Tears fill my eyes.

"You deserve all of this, Ma," I whisper.

"Aw, my love—"

"Is she crying? She better not be crying," Leslie cuts in.

Before I can blink, the rest of my sisters pile into the hug.

"You know, once one of you starts—" Lydia says, her voice wavering.

"The rest of us follow," Layla finishes.

"Goddamn you all," Leslie grumbles, tilting her head back to keep her mascara intact.

A *click, click, click* reminds us we're not alone.

"That was beautiful, fam. Wow." The photographer lowers his camera. "I'm Tiago, Luis' nephew. It's an honor to be a part of this with you all. When you're ready, let's get some family shots and hopefully more of those beautiful smiles instead of tears," he says, winking.

Whitney doesn't miss a beat, appearing at my side as she gracefully hands out bouquets—burgundy and dusty pink roses. The one she hands Mom is twice as big, with red roses mixed in and cascading softly down the front like a waterfall of petals.

Tiago guides us all into position, arranging us around Mom in the center. Leslie, Alfonso, and I are to her left and the twins, Liam, and Aiden are to her right.

He then smacks a hand onto Chase's shoulder. "Why don't you stand behind your girl?"

Chase blinks. "Oh, no. I'm not part of the bridal party."

Tiago hesitates, confused. "Oh, I just thought—"

Mom bumps my arm, whispering, "I don't mind if he's in the pictures."

"You sure?" I ask.

"Only if you are, mamita."

I turn to Chase, butterflies swarming my belly when I meet his gaze. He smiles, and my heart dances in my chest.

Shit.

It shouldn't be this easy—falling this hard, this fast. But with Chase, it just is.

And that's what scares the hell out of me.

How do I do this differently? How do I love without losing pieces of myself in the process?

I gave my heart away too easily once, and I know all too well how much it hurts when it all falls apart. The last time I gave myself to someone, I nearly severed my relationship with my family, and it almost broke me. It wasn't that long ago I pictured forever with someone who only ever used me and let me waste years of my life for his benefit.

Of course I dodged Chase's wedding question earlier. I am definitely not ready to picture our future —no matter how perfect this feels.

But I can picture this. Me and him. Right here. Right now.

Because our battered hearts deserve this perfectly imperfect thing we have found together.

I motion for him to come over. His brows pull together as he tilts his head to the side, confused.

"Get in here, Thor!" Ma calls out and everyone else chimes in, motioning Chase to join us.

Finally, he relents, stopping first to hug Mom before slipping in behind me. His hands settle on my hips, his lips brushing my ear.

"You sure this is okay?" he murmurs.

"With or without the technicalities, Thor," I whisper back, leaning into him.

So what if I'm crazy for being all in this fast? Falling for Chase feels exactly like what I'm meant to be doing right now, and damn, is it worth the risk.

3

CHASE

Once the pictures are done, the rest of the bridal party is sent downstairs to one of the staterooms to wait while Luis and the guests start arriving. Whitney ushers me toward the front of the yacht where the ceremony is set up.

White chairs are lined up in neat rows and there's an arch draped in flowers swaying with the boat. The moment I sit, my shoulders sag, tension draining as I try to steady myself against the slow roll of the deck. My chest tightens with the sway of the boat and I drag a hand over my face.

I've been fighting to distract myself from this constant swaying, breathing slow and steady, but the nausea creeps in. I'm screwed for the rest of the night.

Did I know I suffered from motion sickness before today? Nope. But one thing's for sure—I'll be damned if I lose my lunch in front of Izzy's entire family.

I lean forward, letting my elbows dig into my knees as I lower my head between my legs, hoping to steady myself.

A sudden, heavy slap lands between my shoulder blades, jerking me upright and threatening to send the Yucca fries I inhaled for lunch right overboard.

"Chase, my man!" Luis—Lulu's fiancé—calls out from above me, too damn loud for the way I'm feeling right now. I grit my teeth, swallowing the lump in my throat, and push myself up to meet him.

"Hey, Luis," I say. The effort nearly knocks me back before I shake his hand, but he doesn't seem to notice.

He's dressed sharp in an ivory jacket that matches Lulu's dress, a navy bow tie, and matching pants. His smile is big, easy, with faint crinkles around his eyes like he's has been wearing it all day. The gray in his beard catches the golden light spilling across the deck.

"Today's the big day," I say, nodding toward him. "Congrats, man."

Luis chuckles, shaking his head like he can't believe it himself. "Finally. I feel like I have been waiting forever for this day— since I laid eyes on Lu."

"Yeah, I get that." I nod, my gaze drifting up to the arch, already picturing Izzy there.

Luis' smile stretches wide, the corners of his eyes crinkling deeper. "When you know, you know, right?"

Whitney is suddenly at his side. "Mr. Alvarez, the photographer is ready for you now."

Luis practically bounces on his heels. "Duty calls," he says, clapping me on the shoulder before following her toward the other end of the deck.

Relieved, I sink back into my chair. A stronger wave rolls beneath the hull, slightly shifting the chairs around me, and all I can think is how the hell am I going to survive the next four hours on this boat when I can barely manage a two-second conversation? The deck rocks again, and my stomach turns, heat rushing up my throat but I force it back down. I groan, press my palms into my knees, and squeeze my eyes shut as my pulse pounds in my ears.

Laughter and voices drift around me in English and Spanish, greetings tossed back and forth as guests make their way onboard. All of it blurs into each other while I try to keep it together.

"You're not looking so hot, Thor."

Fuck.

I drag my eyes open, and sure enough, Izzy's best friend, Mya, is standing right in front of me. Her arms crossed over a teal dress like she's been watching me this whole time. Behind her, a man who can only be her husband stands close, his hand resting at the small of her back like it belongs there.

"But you do clean up nice for a gym rat," she teases, then nods beside her. "This is my husband, Kevin."

"Nice to meet you. Do you go by something else other than Thor?" he says, extending a hand toward me.

I huff out a laugh, shaking my head at the nickname before gripping his hand firmly. "Chase."

"Good to finally meet you. My wife has been rooting for you from the start."

"I'll take all the help I can get," I say, managing the faintest grin. The yacht gives another slow roll, my stomach lurching with it. I swallow the lump in my throat as Mya takes the seat next to me, Kevin sliding in beside her.

Mya shoots me a sideways glance, one brow arched. "Don't tell me you don't have sea legs, Thor?"

I force a dry laugh, rubbing a hand over my face. "Wish I knew before today, too."

"Just avoid staring at the water for too long. Focus on the floor or something. My mom swore staring at the waves was like inviting el mareo."

"The what?" I manage.

"The dizziness."

Heat starts to build at the base of my neck, spreading slowly and heavy. I'm sweating from the inside out.

Kevin glances at me, "Aw man, they are going to eat him alive." Kevin chuckles. "Look, it's not too late for you to save yourself, and your dignity and jump off this boat."

"Don't scare him. He'll be fine. I'm texting Izzy right now. Maybe someone has Dramamine."

Kevin snorts. "Don't say I didn't warn you."

"Warn me about what?"

Mya scans the deck as guests start to arrive, then tilts her head toward me. "Look, Lulu has more cousins—and cousins' cousins —than I can keep track of. The older ones are handsy. And not afraid to touch."

"Be prepared to have your cheeks pinched, your biceps squeezed, and your very manhood discussed shamelessly in front of you," Kevin chimes in.

I blink. "Noted."

Mya smirks. "And the younger ones?" She pauses, eyes twinkling before delivering her warning. "Are bold and won't think twice about throwing themselves at you just to see if you'll catch them. Considering how much shit they talked when Izzy was with cara de culo, I can only imagine what they'll have to say about you."

Kevin laughs under his breath. "Translation: smile, nod, and whatever you do—don't let them smell fear."

I let out a slow exhale. "They're going to eat me alive."

Mya grins. "Welcome to the family, Thor."

The band starts up—guitar, percussion, something smooth and steady that rolls over the deck. One by one, the bridal party walks up the aisle.

Lydia and Alfonso, then Layla and Aiden, and finally Liam with Izzy. The second I see her, flowers in hand, the setting sun kissing her skin, my mouth goes dry. And for the first time since boarding, the floor stops spinning. The breeze plays with her hair, tossing strands across her face, but without missing a beat, her eyes lock on mine. Her lips curve just enough to make my heart stutter. She walks past me and takes her place, Leslie right behind her.

I don't know the song, but I feel it in my chest when a soft female voice cuts in, carrying over the deck. Everyone stands as the bride steps into the aisle, yet all I can do is look at Izzy. I don't even notice when when Lulu makes it to Luis, or everyone else sits again. My eyes stay on Izzy, her stare locked on mine. I'd give anything to know what's going through her mind right now, because all I can picture is Izzy standing there instead, promising me the rest of her life.

A tug at my sleeve pulls me back.

"Sit," Mya whispers, a hint of a laugh in her voice.

I blink, realizing I'm the last one still standing. As I drop into my seat, I glance back at Izzy—and she's already watching me, like she caught it too.

The thought slams into me hard. I almost forget about the way my stomach churns.

Almost.

The ceremony moves forward with only a few minor bumps, the constant rocking getting worse as time drags on. At one point, the arch nearly tips over onto the officiant before Whitney and her team re-secure it to the deck, and Lulu stumbles, holding on to Luis for balance.

By the time the ceremony ends, sweat clings to my skin, cold and relentless. The breeze rolls through the darkening sky as the boat finally drifts forward, but it doesn't reach me, not when every slow rock over the waves makes my insides twist.

Now, as the wedding party starts making their way downstairs for the reception, I make a beeline for the restroom to splash cold water on my face and neck, hoping it'll shake off this seasickness and get me through the rest of the night.

I make it a few steps before a pair of hands latch onto my forearm, stopping me in my tracks.

"Hello, tall, blonde y gringo," a voice purrs beside me, smooth as velvet.

I turn to find a woman—mid-forties, sharp brows, bold red lipstick, and a confidence that tells me she gets what she wants. She looks me over, a slow, deliberate once-over that lingers a little too long below my belt.

"How do you know Luis? Coworker? Friend? Doctor?"

Before I can get a word out, Izzy's voice cuts in, sharp and familiar.

"Hi, Tía."

The woman immediately switches gears, pulling Izzy into a hug before placing a hand over her chest with a dramatic sigh.

"Ay, mi amor. How are you doing? I felt so bad for you after what happened with Esteban. Qué pena. You must be so heartbroken. And then for him to turn around and get engaged to that puta? No tiene vergüenza." She shakes her head, then gives Izzy a once-over. "But you look good, mama."

I catch the way Izzy's jaw tightens for a split second before she smooths it over.

"I'm good, Tía. Actually, better than I have been in a long time." Her hand slides into mine. "And this is Chase. He's with me."

The woman—Sylvia—blinks once. Then twice. Then slowly takes in our clasped hands.

"Ohhh!" Her brows shoot up as she looks at us, a slow smile tugging at her lips. "Okay, I see you, little Izzy. You are your momma's daughter." She chuckles. "You know what she always says—"

"Please, don't—" Izzy mutters, turning away.

"The best way to get over a man is under the next one." She claps her hands together, grinning. "And girl, did you upgrade."

She nods approvingly, then turns to me, her expression shifting ever so slightly.

"Don't be a pendejo like the last one, or I swear..."

I don't know what that 'P' word means, but I know it's not good. Pretty sure I've heard Lulu and Leslie use it when talking about Aiden and Alfonso's dad. So yeah—definitely not good.

She pats me on the shoulder once—firm, almost threatening—then spins on her heels and saunters off like she didn't just verbally bodycheck me.

"Sorry about that."

"I thought your mom didn't have any siblings?"

"She doesn't, but they grew up together." Izzy studies me for a moment, then tilts her head. "Mya texted me. Are you feeling okay?"

I exhale, rubbing the back of my neck. "I'll be okay. Just need some water."

"Come on." She leads me down a narrow hallway to a small room that suddenly feels too tight.

"Sit," she orders, pointing to the edge of the bed before disappearing into the bathroom.

I sink into the bed, closing my eyes as the boat rocks beneath me, my stomach doing its best to keep up.

The rush of running water hits my ears, followed by he soft rustle of movement nearby. Then, cool pressure presses against my burning forehead. I groan low as Izzy's fingers brush gently over my skin with a towel, making the swaying fade for just a second.

"Better?" she asks.

I nod faintly, the room settling for a moment. "Always better with you," I whisper.

"Want me to take your mind off it?"

My eyes snap open just in time to catch the teasing glint in hers.

Before I can respond, Izzy swings a leg over my lap, settling onto me as a different kind of heat rushes through my body.

"Izzy—" My voice is strained, though I'm not entirely sure if it's from nausea or the way she's pressing against me.

"What?" she asks innocently, fingers trailing over my shoulders before dragging down my chest. "It's a distraction, isn't it?"

My hands instinctively find her waist. "Yeah, I think it's working a little too well."

She smirks, leaning in until her lips graze the edge of my jaw. "Good. Just focus on me," she whispers before pressing her lips to mine.

The rocking of the boat disappears, replaced by the slow, deliberate heat of her body pressed against mine—the squeeze of her thighs around my sides, the teasing roll of her hips. My hands tighten on her waist, instinctive, reflexive, like holding onto her is the only thing keeping me grounded.

She starts to pull away, and I lean forward, not ready to lose her touch just yet, as she rolls her hips one last time, dragging a low groan out of me before pushing up onto her knees.

My fingers flex against her, resisting the space she's putting between us, but she only smirks, brushing my hands away while she trails down my body. Her warmth lingers even as she slides between my legs.

My breath catches in my throat as she reaches for my belt, fingers working the buckle open with ease. The *clink* barely registers over the pounding in my ears, the steady throb of my pulse drowning out everything else. Then my zipper drags down, the fabric loosening around me, and the second the pressure eases, heat rolls through me.

My hand slides into her hair, smoothing it back as I look down at her, my voice rough. "How long do we have?"

Izzy glances up, eyes dark, as her fingers slip beneath my waistband, nails grazing my skin. "Maybe ten minutes."

I shake my head while she tugs my briefs down just enough to free my already throbbing cock. Her fingers wrap around me. Her thumb brushing over the tip before she strokes me slowly. It pulls a sharp hiss from between my teeth.

Definitely not enough time. Not for the way I want her.

Then her lips part, and before I can get another word out, she wraps them around me and sinks down.

A ragged curse rips from my throat, my head tipping back as heat crashes through me, wiping out any thought of time, the reception, or the damn boat swaying beneath us.

Her mouth is everything—warm, wet, and perfect, her tongue teasing along the underside. Fuck. She makes me feel so good.

She takes me deeper, her hand wrapping around what she can't fit. My fingers flex in her hair, not pushing, just holding, trying to ground myself as she works me over, slow and steady, like she's got all the time in the world.

She hums around me, and fuck—the vibration sends a sharp pulse of pleasure straight through me, making my grip tighten. My thighs grow rigid beneath her. She knows exactly what she's doing, dragging this out, taking her time even though we don't have much of it.

I groan, my hips jerking involuntarily as she flicks her tongue over the tip, her hand stroking in perfect rhythm, like she's hell-bent on ruining me.

A curse slips under my breath, control slipping as the need to be inside her takes over.

I pull her up, turning her onto her hands and knees. I move faster than I should with the boat still rocking—but the second I'm behind her, everything steadies.

She gasps as I push her dress up around her waist.

She doesn't waste a second reaching back to hook her fingers into the side of her underwear, dragging the black lace down. I follow the movement, my hands gliding over her thighs, tracing the curve of her legs as the fabric slips lower— over her calves— until it catches at her heels.

Reaching into my back pocket, I pull out the condom I stuffed there earlier—because the way Izzy and I have been going at it, best to be prepared—and tear it open fast before shoving my pants down to my knees.

Then I step in behind her. My hands grip her hips, dragging her back against me, guiding her between my thighs, her back flush to my chest. Her body open, ready, waiting.

I slide my fingers over her wetness—teasing, testing—circling her clit, making her gasp.

"Chase—" she whispers, her voice of need.

I press my mouth to the back of her shoulder, as she leans into me, her body fitting against mine. My hands flex against her hips as I line myself up and push in, slow and steady, sinking deep until I'm buried inside her.

A sharp moan slips from her lips, her fingers gripping my thigh as she adjusts around me—tight, hot, perfect.

My forehead drops against the side of her neck, forcing myself to breathe, to wait, to let her catch up.

But she rolls her hips, exhaling hard. "We don't have much time, remember?"

A slow, wicked grin tugs at my mouth.

"Yeah. I remember."

And for the first time all day, I don't feel sick—I feel steady. Grounded in *her*.

I pull back, my hands tightening on her hips before driving into her again and again, until she's choking on her gasp, arching against me, and meeting every thrust with a desperate push back.

And fuck me. Any control I thought I had left?

Gone.

Until her core is squeezing me tight and her whole body is shuddering beneath me. And suddenly she feels too far away. I shove a few buttons of my dress shirt open, dragging it over my head before slowly guiding her up as I tug her dress the rest of the way over her shoulders and head. Her warm back presses against my chest, her entire body loose from her release. She cries out—loud enough that anyone nearby definitely hears.

"Shh...I'm so close, baby."

I drop my mouth to the curve of her neck, tasting the sweet heat of her skin while I slip my fingers over her swollen clit. I pull her tighter against me, like I'm afraid she'll slip out of my arms if I let go. I drive into her harder, faster, deeper while she writhes against me.

Finally, I lose whatever control I had left, giving her everything I've been trying and failing to keep contained.

4

———

IZZY

"Do you think anyone will notice?"

Chase chuckles as I wipe a finger under my eyes, dragging a streak of mascara with me. The tiny mirror confirms it —I look thoroughly wrecked.

"Define 'notice,'" he says, narrowing his eyes as he tugs his shirt on.

"My hair's a mess and I'm pretty sure my dress is on backwards," I say, frowning as I search for the side slit I know was there before.

"It's not backwards," he murmurs, stepping in behind me. I lean back against him as his hand trails down my hip until his fingers find the skin of my thigh through the slit. His hands slip inside, gliding up the bare skin of my thigh, tugging the fabric back into place where it belongs.

"Good to know my little distraction helped and you're feeling all better." I pry myself away from him and slide my feet into my heels.

"How about—" he trails off as he dips his head to the curve of my neck, lips tickling my skin when he kisses along my neck "—we stay... in here... and continue this distraction?"

My eyes are captivated by the mirror in front of us, the couple reflected there, suspended in a moment where time has stopped just for them. His lips linger at my neck, unhurried, like he has nowhere else to be—like he's memorizing me, worshiping skin that's been doubted, questioned, and hurt before.

"Very tempting, Thor," I say just as the low pulse of music vibrates faintly through the cabin walls. "But the reception is definitely in full swing by now."

"You mean the one everyone's definitely noticed we've been missing from?"

"You're right." I hesitate, already running through the fastest way to make the fact that we had sex in the middle of my mother's wedding reception look less obvious. "I'll go out first and you wait five minutes, okay?" I don't wait for him to answer before pushing the door open. I steal one quick look back—just one—before stepping out, the door clicking shut behind me.

I lean my head back against the door, and for a second, I almost give in to the urge to skip the entire reception and lock us in here for the rest of the night... until Mya's voice cuts in from down the hall.

"Are you done defiling the boat, or should I circle back?"

I blush, covering my face with both hands. "I feel too damn good to even try to deny it."

"Good," she says, her heels clicking closer. She's wearing a long-sleeve, indigo dress with an asymmetrical hem that catches the hallway light. "Because you're a terrible liar."

I pull her into a hug and mumble against her shoulder. "You look amazing."

"And you look freshly ruined," she whispers back, then pulls away, throwing me a look that says, *I know exactly what you did, and I'd have done the same.*

"Come on, I told him to wait five minutes before walking out." I loop my arm through hers and drag her toward the main deck.

She snorts. "Because that'll make it less obvious."

"Better than walking out at the exact same time."

"Please. Everyone's going to clock it the second they see you two together, and I want a front row seat."

We enter the reception area as guitar strings and a soft percussion spill from the small live band tucked near the edge of the main deck. My body instantly reacts to the undeniable bachata rhythm my grandmother raised us on. It is my mom's way of having her here today, at least in spirit. Shoulders rolling side to side, hips swaying in that gentle rocking way. The boat shifts beneath my feet a little stronger than before, but the music smooths it out. Even Mya falls into the same beat, hands lifting in front of her as she moves to the music. My eyes bounce around the room, landing on the wedding guests swaying in their seats or clustered at the open bar, their voices overlapping in a mix of Spanish and English.

"There's Kevin," she says, tipping her chin forward to the front of the room. I can't see his tight curls and tall frame from where I'm standing, even in heels. What I can see is the inevitable sea of people we'll have to push through to get there.

So much for slipping in unnoticed, I think to myself.

My stomach dips at the thought. I already know exactly how this is going to go. I haven't seen some of these people in years, and even then, all anyone could talk about was when Estaban would propose.

I shove the thought aside as quick as it comes and brace myself as we head straight into the crowd.

We barely make it a few steps before I'm pulled into hugs and conversations. Every single one of them with *that* look in their eyes, thinly veiled pity like I'm some walking cautionary tale. I am measured against the women in my family—my body, my age, and the unspoken countdown they all seem to hear.

A few steps forward.

"Ay mi niña, we thought it would be you getting married by now."

I'm twenty-six, not expired. I hold my smile, teeth clenching behind it.

Another hug. Another pause. Another—

"What a shame about the breakup."

We try again, inching toward the table before someone else catches my arm.

"Izzy, have you lost weight? Are you taking those shots? Mi comadre's prima is on it and—"

I shake my head, but Mya steps in before I can say anything else.

"Actually, Izzy doesn't need that. Her new man is a personal trainer."

I whip my head toward her as she flashes my mom's co-worker, a.k.a Gossip Queen, the smuggest look I've ever seen.

"Que-que?" she sputters, her eyes darting around the room as if she'd be able to find him.

"It was so good to see you," I say, tugging Mya along with me.

Once we are out of earshot, I bump Mya's shoulder. "You know what you just did, right?"

"Sorry, girl, but I could not stand there and listen to their nonsense for one more second. Looking at you like your life is over."

"I should have stayed in that damn room."

Mya leans in, and I can practically hear the smirk on her lips. "They pity you now—wait 'till they see the way Thor looks at you. Se van a explotar con envidia."

I snort. "Well, then I hope they're sitting front row."

We finally reach our table—front and center, right on the edge of the dance floor, directly across from the bride and groom's empty sweetheart table. Kevin and Layla are already there, while Lydia, Leslie, and the rest of them fill the table beside ours. Kevin stands when he sees us, flashing a grin.

"Look who finally decided to show up," he says, pulling me into a quick hug.

"We were handling a situation," Mya says, taking the seat beside him and smoothing her dress.

Kevin settles back into his chair, a knowing smile firmly in place. "You were hooking up on the yacht."

"Kevin!" Mya and I blurt out together. My eyes dart to Layla, who just rolls her eyes at us.

"Nasties," she says, pushing back her chair as she stands.

Kevin lifts his glass, unbothered. "Hey, I'm not judging. Just jealous. Three years married, and I still can't get away with that kind of timing."

"Because you're loud," Mya deadpans, a smile tugging at the corner of her mouth.

Kevin leans back, grinning. "I prefer memorable."

Mya gives him a look. "That's one word for it."

The DJ's voice cuts through the music.

"All right, everyone. Vamo' comenzar y celebrar esta noche de amor! If you're not in your seats yet, go ahead and find them."

Scattered cheers ripple across the deck as people shuffle to their tables, drinks in hand, heels clicking against the wood floor. The opening chords of "El Amor" by Tito El Bambino begin as a soft spotlight settles over the double doors where the photographer waits, camera lifted.

I scan the room for Chase, turning and craning my neck. He should've been out here by now. My stomach twists. What if the sea sickness came back?

The double doors swing open, and clapping breaks out across the deck only to stutter to a stop. Instead of the bride and groom, it's Chase. Caught in the bright spotlight. Completely out of place.

Oh my god.

I'm moving before I fully register it, pushing my chair back and quickly crossing the dance floor. Whitney appears behind him, headset on, muttering into it and shaking her head at the sight of Chase in front of her. His eyes flicker toward her before turning back and finding mine. Relief hits his face instantly as he steps out of the spotlight and straight toward me.

Our hands meet, and I turn, guiding him back to our table before the moment can stretch any longer. The eyes of every guest follow us as we make our way across the floor.

The DJ's mic crackles. "Y este payaso?"

A few laughs break out, and heat flashes up my neck. I reach him, my hand sliding into his just as his other hand presses against my lower back urging us forward.

"I can't believe that just happened," he mutters behind me.

We reach our table and Kevin pats him on the back.

"All right, mi gente, let's try this again. Por primera vez, let's welcome Mr. and Mrs. Pena-Alvarez!"

The deck erupts in applause and whistles. Around us, drinks are raised and cheers ripple through the crowd. Mom and Luis step out hand in hand, grinning like teenagers, waving as they make their way to the center of the dance floor.

The music shifts, rising into the soft guitar and smooth rhythm of "El Amor" as Luis pulls Mom close, their hands finding each other easily, like they've been dancing to it their whole lives. They sway together, hips moving in sync.

Beside me, Chase's hand brushes mine before he links our fingers. Then, without a word, he tugs me in front of him and wraps his arms around my waist, pulling me back against his chest. I let myself settle into the space he's created—warm, quiet, safe.

"They look happy," he murmurs, his voice low against my ear.

"They are," I say, watching the way Mom laughs when Luis spins her. "She deserves this."

He presses a kiss to the side of my head, and something stirs deep in my chest—warm and terrifying all at once.

I think of his question from earlier, when we were getting ready.

Is that how you would want to do it?

A wedding without all the fuss.

No. I'd want it all. The people, the chaos, the noise.

It hits me then—how real this is getting.

In just one month.

I love you.

And a whole future taking shape in front of me.

My body tenses.

The thought slips in, uninvited.

Because I've felt this before. I've pictured forever once—only to have it ripped away the moment I let myself believe it was real. I shut the thought down before it can grow roots and hold still, like if I don't move, the fear won't notice me.

He loves me, I remind myself.

He's not him. He's nothing like my ex.

But my body doesn't believe me. Not after all the looks tonight. The backhanded comments. The pity. The whispers.

And now here I am—held by someone who actually shows up for me, who sees me, who makes it all feel possible again—and all I can think about is how fast it could disappear.

So, I don't say anything. I don't pull away either. I let the music fill the silence. Let his hands ground me to this love that feels so real. Because tonight, who I am with Chase is the only thing holding the pieces in place.

5

CHASE

"I'm gonna be sick," I mutter, dropping into the nearest chair and gripping the edge as another wave of nausea rolls through me. It hasn't even been an hour since dinner and this boat has me rethinking every life choice I've ever made. The boat rolls beneath me again, sharper than before, and impossible to ignore.

"Aw, shit, someone tell Izzy to come get her man!" Leslie's voice rings out from above, her voice carrying through the reception room.

"Maybe Whitney has puke bags?" Someone calls out next.

"Puke bags?" I immediately start shaking my head in refusal, my stomach churning violently. A cold sweat breaks out across my skin as I struggle to keep my composure. I push to my feet to pace, but the constant motion sends me stumbling back into my seat.

I glance down at my watch and squeeze my eyes shut. The frustration and embarrassment clawing at me is almost as bad as the nausea.

A reassuring hand lands on my knee and without opening my eyes, I know it's her. I breathe in through my nose, catching the soft trace of her perfume—light and sweet, like summer. The tension in my stomach eases, just a little.

"This isn't how I pictured the night going," I say, tipping my head back toward the ceiling.

"You are giving a lot more Hulk than Thor right now." She presses her palm against my cheek, the touch distracting me for a second.

A soft chuckle slips out of me as I force my eyes open, landing on Izzy in front of me. She leans in so close her breath brushes my lips.

"Maybe you just need another distraction?" she mutters. The faint scent of alcohol wafts across my face. My eyes bounce to hers, warm and a little glassy. Her smile wobbles—just enough to give her away. She's definitely a little more than buzzed, and definitely trying to act like she's not.

"How much have you had to drink?" I ask, pushing my own discomfort as far down as I can and tugging her gently down onto my lap. She doesn't hesitate like she used to, draping her arms around my shoulder, her fingers brushing the back of my neck.

"Not that much." She giggles, and I have to turn my head to the side, pushing down another wave of nausea as she settles into the crook of my neck.

I clear my throat as a knot, not at all like the seasickness, forms in my stomach, squeezing tight. Nora flashes through my mind, unwelcome. I hold Izzy close, screwing my eyes shut.

Izzy is nothing like my mother.

She isn't a raging alcoholic.

She is a beautiful young woman, enjoying herself.

She isn't trying to drown out her past...

...or is she?

No.

But she *did* seem a little off earlier, and again after the bride and groom's first dance.

"Izzy!" Gisela—one of her cousins I met earlier—stops in front of us, shaking a yellow prescription bottle in her hand. "Someone said you were looking for something for motion sickness."

Izzy lifts her head, eyes flicking over me with a crooked smile. "My thunder god isn't looking too good."

Gisela scoffs, holding out the bottle to me. "We can't have that, especially not when he hasn't even shown us his moves on the dance floor yet."

"You're a lifesaver," I say, relief washing over me at the thought of not feeling like this much longer. Plus, it'll help me take care of a tipsy Izzy.

"Of course. Welcome to the family, Thor," she says with a wave, already walking away.

Izzy slides off my lap and reaches for a glass of water from the table, pressing it into my hand before I can ask. I down two capsules like my life depends on it, because right now, it kind of does.

I don't miss the fact that Izzy is here, making sure I'm okay, and I feel like a dumbass for letting myself even get a little annoyed. The realization settles in slowly. Hell, it probably wasn't Izzy at all but the seasickness amplifying everything. I make a quiet promise to myself to be better. She deserves better than my old reflexes.

The DJ's voice cuts through the speakers. "Just heard from the captain that we've still got time before we head back to shore, so vamo' migente. Let's fill this dance floor!"

The unmistakable beat of the Cha-Cha Slide kicks in, pulling everyone to their feet. Izzy turns toward me, eyes bright with excitement, cha-cha'ing in front of me as she nods toward the dance floor.

Not quite ready to get on my feet just yet, I motion my head. "You have fun."

"I love you," she mouths, forming a heart with her hands as she walks backward onto the dance floor.

A smile tugs at my lips, my heart tightening in the best way. She turns and squeezes in next to Mya and her sister, Lydia. Everyone but Leslie is barefoot, having ditched their heels right after dinner. My grin stays locked in place as they dance, each of them gliding and shuffling to their own rhythm.

The relentless rolling in my stomach has finally eased up, but I remain in my seat. I shake my head, clearing away wandering thoughts that had dragged me down earlier. I don't know where they came from, but they can go right back to whatever dark corner of my mind it conjured itself up from.

My fucked up past and Nora's bullshit call are exactly where they belong. Behind me. They don't get to follow me here and dictate this relationship or the future I want so badly I can taste it.

Izzy glances back at me from the dance floor, laughing and

stumbling through the steps. She catches me watching and lifts a brow. "Come on," she mouths, waving me over.

I push myself up from my chair, legs a little unsteady but manageable, and nod. Thankful as fuck to finally feel human again.

Yeah. I'm good, I say to myself as I start moving towards her.

And the future with her tastes so fucking sweet.

As I step onto the edge of the dance floor, the music pulses through my feet. The small group around Izzy, made up of Mya, Kevin, and her little sisters cheer when I slide in beside her. She laughs as everyone stomps in unison, and I try to get my footing right but go into a slide instead of a criss-cross. I catch the next beat too late and correct myself again, shoulders loosening as I follow the next call, still half a step behind, but still laughing with everyone. I feel like I belong—like these are my people and I've finally found where I fit.

The song transitions into the next one, a more upbeat Latin rhythm followed by a high-pitched voice that belts out through the speakers. This triggers a response from everyone but me, shouting "Bésame!" Bodies sway from side to side as I stand in the middle of it like a tree in a windstorm. Rooted to the dance floor, everyone swirls around me. With no instructions to guide me here, I'm not sure what the hell to do with myself, so I sway my shoulders side to side and try to stay out of the way.

Izzy luckily reaches for me, her hands sliding along my waist and pulling me closer as her hips sway to the beat. Sweat clings to her forehead, her face flushed and glowing as she smiles up at me. Her edge from earlier about the wedding is gone. She's happy and carefree. I want her to feel like this always, preferably without alcohol.

"I don't know how to dance to this," I say, leaning down so she can hear me over the music.

She laughs and takes my hands, placing one at her lower back and guiding the other to hers. "You don't have to," she says, "Just feel it."

She shifts her weight, hips swaying side to side, slow and easy, coaxing me along with her. I follow, a beat behind at first, until the movement starts to make sense. Less steps, more convincing my hips to cooperate.

"Okay, Papi Thor!" Lulu appears at my side, bumping her hip into mine. "I guess you are invited to the cookout after all!"

"Wait," I say, laughing, "I wasn't already invited?"

"No way, Thor!" Lulu says, as Luis spins her.

"You gotta earn that spot. Let's see what you got," Luis adds.

Before I can respond, Kevin slides in beside them, grinning. "She's not kidding."

Suddenly all eyes are on me as they start to circle me—clapping, chanting, hyping me up. The music changes, the beat dropping heavier, faster, bass thudding through the deck as Spanish lyrics spill out through the speakers. The crowd erupts like this is what they've been waiting for.

"Thor! Thor! Thor!" they chant, laughing, the circle tightening as I glance up at Izzy, panic flashing in my eyes for half a second. She laughs, mouthing *sorry*, still clapping and bobbing her head to the beat.

I do what any person who's spent too much time on social media does, bending my knees and rolling my hips forward and back like the online dances I've seen trending.

The reaction is instant as they all cheer me on, but I barely have time to register it before a woman jumps in front of me, bending down low and dancing way too close. I quickly avert my eyes and take a step back.

When I look up, Izzy isn't laughing.

She's standing a few feet away, hurt flashing across her face before she spins around, storming off in the opposite direction.

My heart sinks and my feet automatically carry me after her.

"Izzy—hey," I call, quickly catching up to her. "What's wrong?"

I reach for her arm, fingers closing around it.

She yanks free. "Funny," she says bitterly. "You didn't seem in a hurry to stop *her*."

I blink, frowning. "What?"

A quiet laugh almost slips out. *That's what this is.* She's jealous? Of some random girl?

"I don't want to keep you from your new dance partner," she adds, already turning away like she's done with this conversation. Done with me.

The smile falls from my lips.

She sways, and I'm already stepping in, catching her by the arm before she loses her balance.

"That's not what happened," I say quietly, my grip loosening on her arm but not letting go.

"Sure it's not. Just forget it."

"No," I push, stepping in front of her. "Talk to me."

She lets out a sharp breath, "It's nothing, okay."

Yeah. Right.

"Izzy—"

"I said it's nothing." Her voice is tight.

Her sharp, defensive tone hits too close to home but I push it down, forcing my mind not to go there.

"If it were nothing, we would still be enjoying the rest of the reception right now."

Her eyes snap up to mine.

"Then what do you want me to say?" she shoots back.

"The truth."

She laughs under her breath, shaking her head. "Like how comfortable you looked dancing with someone else."

"I wasn't," I say, stepping closer. "I didn't even know what the hell was happening until she was already in my space."

"But you didn't stop it."

"I stepped back."

"After," she says, crossing her arms.

I drag a hand down my face. "I'm trying here, Izzy."

She stills.

"I'm trying to be your boyfriend here—" I say, quieter now, "—but I swear you're bracing for the exit."

Her jaw flexes. For a second, I think she's going to push me away again—walk off, shut me out before things get too real.

But she doesn't.

Instead, her shoulders slump, the fight draining out of her as she steps forward, resting her forehead against my chest.

"I just..." Her voice catches.

My chest tightens. "Just what?"

She swallows, fingers curling into my shirt.

"If I'm already expecting it," she whispers, "you can't surprise me with goodbye."

The words land heavy, sinking straight into my chest.

I don't know what to say to that. Not without tearing everything open—right here, on a staircase, at her mother's wedding.

But damn it, one minute she's choosing me without hesitation, and the next, she's pulling back like she doesn't trust herself to be happy.

She's drunk.

And still—this doesn't feel like the alcohol talking.

I wrap my arms around her anyway, holding her steady while the boat rocks beneath us. The pain she's still carrying presses between us like a third presence I can't touch or fix.

I don't pull away.

But for the first time tonight, I don't know if holding her is enough.

6

————

IZZY

"*I'm trying to be your boyfriend here, but I swear you're bracing for the exit.*

My eyes snap open and I am filled with immediate regret as harsh light floods my vision. Bright. Unforgiving. It seeps through the bare window of my apartment bedroom.

My stomach drops before the rest of me catches up.

Chase's words from last night echo louder than the pounding in my head. Squeezing my eyes shut, I tug the comforter over my head, seeking refuge while the jagged pieces of last night start replaying on a loop I didn't ask for. I drank enough to earn a hangover—but not enough to forget exactly how stupid I acted.

God. Why do I do this to myself?

The sound of my bedroom door creaking open interrupts my spiraling thoughts. I peel the bedding back slightly, just enough to see Chase stepping into my bedroom, looking like he walked straight out of one of my spicy romance novels, which is absolutely unfair considering I currently feel like a dehydrated gremlin with regret.

He's shirtless. Obviously. And wearing the retro blue Marvel pajama pants I bought him, with Thor's hammer printed all over them. Of course they hang low on his hips. And of course, my eyes betray me immediately, zeroing in on that stupid, perfect V-line which disappears beneath the waistband.

And as if he isn't perfect enough already, in this man's hand is a hot plate of pancakes. Hunger rises within me for the pancakes, for him, but it twists into guilt just as quickly. He has practically spent his entire life taking care of Nora because of her drinking, and now here he is, doing it again with me.

My stomach flips. Not from my slight hangover—well, maybe a little—but from the impending conversation I know we need to have but would rather avoid. The kind where he's calm and sober and remembers every word I slurred out, and I have to sit there and explain myself like I wasn't just drunk and emotional at a wedding.

I tuck myself back under the blanket, aware of him on the other side, giving me a moment. I mean, he is here with breakfast in bed. Maybe if I don't bring it up, we can just pretend it never happened...

Maybe we can slip back into the little bubble we built, when everything still felt light—before I let my insecurities mess it up.

The bed suddenly dips beside me with his weight. He tugs the blanket away and I'm caught in his gaze, those green eyes searching my face for answers I don't even know the questions to.

"Why are you hiding from me, Izzy?" He asks, his voice low. Not accusing. Just... honest.

"Because you shouldn't be here taking care of me right now. You've spent enough of your life taking care of others." My eyes drop to the blanket between us.

He reaches out and captures my chin with his thumb, gently forcing my eyes back up to meet his. "I want to take care of you. Nothing is going to change that."

"Well you shouldn't. I'm a grown woman who should suffer the consequences and learn her lesson." I cover myself back up under the blanket. "What if you grow to resent me and compare me to Nora?"

"You and these what ifs," he replies. "I'm not a fan of alcohol but that's my shit to deal with." His fingers tug down on my blanket and his eyes lock in on mine, steady. "I'm not here to control you or make you feel bad for enjoying yourself. You getting a little carried away doesn't make you an alcoholic." He pauses, his brows furrowing slightly. "I'll work through it, however it makes me feel. I promise."

"So, it does make you feel some type of way?" I tug the sheets back over my face.

"Yeah, I guess it does, but you aren't Nora, Izzy."

That should make me feel better...but it doesn't.

I got drunk. I avoided everything I didn't want to feel. And took it out on him.

Am I really any better than her?

"I'm crazy in love with you, remember?" he says, his voice soft.

"Only because you were dropped on your head," I mumble.

The bed shifts again as he slips under the covers beside me, invading my blanketed cocoon. Lying semi-naked in just my bra and underwear, he slides the palm of his hand along my belly, my body instinctively sucking in a breath at his touch. His bare chest presses against my side as he peppers my shoulder and neck with soft kisses, sending a shiver down my spine. My hips arch back automatically as I tilt my head to the side, giving his lips better access.

"I'm in love with you, Izzy. Stop trying to convince yourself otherwise," he whispers in my ear, gently tugging on my earlobe with his teeth. His fingers skate across the hem of my lace underwear. My body hums with the anticipation of his touch and heat pools between my thighs.

Maybe this is easier.

Easier than talking.

Easier than admitting how much this — *us* — scares me.

In a few seconds, he's over me, tearing the bedding off of us and tossing it behind him, leaving my half naked body bare for him to see in the light of day. I force my eyes on his, heated and intent, as they slowly trace a path down my body. I fight the constant urge to cover myself, muffling the familiar whispers in my head about my body. I don't want to hide, not when he's looking at me like this. I want to be seen, touched, and devoured by this man.

I bite my bottom lip and part my legs, inviting him closer without a word.

"What do you want, Izzy?"

"Just you, Thor," I say with a small smile, knowing exactly what he'll say next.

He shakes his head. "Not Thor when I'm in between you, babe." His hands slide slowly over my thighs.

"Chase, please." I wrap my legs around him, pulling him closer.

"Izzy, are you awake ye-" Liam calls out, bursting into my bedroom. Chase barely has time to react before we are both scrambling, eyes wide, to cover my naked body.

"What are you guys doing?" he asks, his brows pulling together.

"Nothing, just—" Chase responds, searching for an answer as he stares down at me. I shake my head, racking my brain for words.

"Fixing the bed," I blurt out.

Chase scrunches his face at my answer.

"Naked?" Liam asks.

"Not naked!" Chase shouts.

"Liam, could you give us a minute, please?" I plead, burying my face in Chase's chest and shaking my head at myself for completely forgetting I promised Liam he could stay with me while mom is on her honeymoon.

"I'll just close the door," Liam says, already backing out, "but maybe lock it next time you guys are fixing the bed."

"Thank you," Chase and I say in unison.

Once the sound of the door clicks shut, Chase and I breathe out a sigh of relief before falling into laughter.

The laughter fades a little too quickly.

Because we both know we didn't actually *finish* that conversation.

"I forgot all about him."

"So did I," he says. "And I've spent all morning feeding and entertaining him."

"I guess we will have to finish this when he leaves then."

"And when is that again?"

"Thursday."

Chase drops his face into the crook of my neck before shifting his weight onto his arms and rolling onto his side beside mine. I stand, grabbing my robe from its spot on my desk chair and tying it around myself.

"So," he says, "Are we going to talk about last night?"

Of course, he still wants to talk about it. And here I was hoping we could brush it off as me being tipsy. His words replay in my mind anyway.

...you keep bracing for the exit.

"About what?" I ask, busying my hands with my hair.

"Okay," he says, though his jaw tightens like it's not okay at all.

Because I am bracing for the exit—waiting for him to leave, for this to be over.

Not because Chase has done anything wrong—but because I know what happens when I let myself go all in.

Five years of loving the wrong person—and then losing it all—taught me that.

But every day I find myself standing on the edge of this beautiful thing we've found. I want to dive in, but something in me hesitates–like it hasn't forgotten what it cost me the last time I gave in to my heart.

"Really?" He asks, the sharpness in his tone making me spin around.

He sits up in bed, leaning against the bumpy surface of the popcorn style wall behind him.

"Okay," he says.

My eyebrows rise in question, expecting confrontation but instead, he reaches for the plate of pancakes beside him, bringing it to his chest and cutting a piece with the side of the fork.

My stomach rumbles, reminding me how hungry I am right now.

"I thought those were for me?"

He doesn't respond. Instead, he pops the fork into his mouth and cocks his head to the side, while slowly chewing *my* pancakes.

We stare at each other, eyes locked in a silent battle until, a second later, his soften. He stabs another piece with his fork and extends his arm toward me. And because I am a sucker for pancakes, I shuffle over to his side and accept his offering. His eyes dart to my lips as I wrap them around the cold metal, lingering for a moment before he pulls the fork away.

"You know you can talk to me, Izzy," he says softly.

I nod, swallowing down the piece of buttery goodness. "What do you want me to say? I had a little bit too much to drink and I said some things I didn't mean. I'm sorry. I was drunk.

"Okay," he says, placing the plate on the nightstand.

He stands, taking a single step forward until he's right in front of me—close enough that I have to tilt my head up to meet his eyes.

"And I know better than anyone," he says, quieter now, his eyes holding mine, "that there's always some truth to a drunk mind."

I swallow the lump in my throat as he continues, "Just promise me you haven't let someone else's mistakes decide this for us." His hand comes up, brushing my cheek—gentle, almost hesitant.

The way his hooded eyes search mine makes my heart ache.

My head shakes automatically, the word *no* stuck on my tongue as guilt twists inside me. I lean into his touch, my hand coming up to rest over his. "I promise you that's not what's happening."

Although it kind of is, but I hate that I made him feel like I wasn't sure about us. And I'll be damned if I let my ex take anything else from me.

"Okay," he says, a small smile touching his lips.

He kisses the top of my head before taking a step back.

"That's it?" I ask quietly.

"Yeah," he says simply. "I'm not here to punish you. I'm here to love you."

And somehow that makes it worse.

Because all I can think about is how losing him will ruin me for good.

My heart dips as I force a smile, ignoring the whisper in my head that nothing this good ever lasts. I rise onto my tiptoes and press a soft kiss to Chase's lips.

"You're pretty perfect, you know that?"

"Whatever you want me to be, babe. Perfect, crazy... a personal trainer." A crooked smile tugs on his lips.

My lips twitch. "Hey!" I smack his chest. "Too soon, but you *are* almost a real trainer now."

He takes a step back, rubbing a hand over the top of his head. "If you and Damon have your way."

"What does that mean?"

"Nothing. I just don't want to let you down."

"This isn't about me. This is about you taking this passion you have and turning it into something more fulfilling than the job you fell into at sixteen. This certification is just paperwork, anyway. You already train me. Thanks to you, I have come to hate the gym a little less now."

"A little less?" he asks, arching a brow.

"I mean..." I bite my lip glancing up at him, "I do come for the eye candy."

"Oh, I know what you come for."

"Chase!" I laugh out loud. "I'm taking a shower. A cold one," I say, turning around and leaving him chuckling behind me. "And I'm coming back for my pancakes!"

We move on like everything's fine.

But it's not.

It's just... quiet for now.

After a quick shower, cold pancakes, and some time snuggled up with my boys on the secondhand couch I found on Marketplace, we decide to head to the Philly Zoo.

It's surprisingly not as packed as I had imagined, which is a total switch from yesterday's Saturday frenzy by the port. With summer right around the corner, I can almost taste the freedom it promises. I am so ready for a break longer than a few days, one that won't be filled with lesson planning or grading. A few months ago, I didn't even want to imagine what this summer would look like for me. It's the first time in years I won't be spending summer with my ex and his family. No more traveling, no more living at his beck and call, playing assistant, maid, and cook.

"This was nice," Chase says, tearing me from my thoughts. We're seated on a bench in the underwater viewing center at Penguin Point, while Liam enjoys his ice cream.

I lean back into Chase's outstretched arm behind me, an effortless smile tugging at my lips. This *is* nice and I can easily imagine what our summers will look like together. My heart flutters in my chest as I picture it, *picture us*. Easy mornings tangled in each other's arms, laughing in the gym as I try to avoid death by cardio, and nights filled with a peace in my heart I've never known before.

I never knew love could be like this. Feel so safe. Like an oasis that belongs to only us.

"I can't believe you've never been to the zoo, Thor. My dad used to take me all the time," Liam says, inhaling the last of his chocolate ice cream.

Liam's dad really isn't half bad. He works construction and keeps crazy hours, but when he does show up, he actually tries to be present, which is a lot more than can be said for most sperm donors.

He and Mom were never really together. Just one night, one celebration that turned into a lifetime commitment. He tried to pursue something more after, but Mom could tell he was trying to build a life out of obligation, not love.

Loving someone because you have to isn't the same as loving them because you can't see yourself without them.

"What did you and your dad do when you were little, then?" Liam asks curiously as he licks ice cream from his fingers.

"Eh," Chase moves his arm from behind me and sits forward, resting his elbows on his knees in thought. "He took me fishing once, but he left not that long after."

"Oh," Liam responds. "Did he die like Izzy's dad?"

My father died before I was born in a motorcycle accident, and as much as that hurt and confused me when I was younger, at least I had my mom and Mama, her mom.

"Nope." Chase's eyes stay fixed on the glass in front of us, penguins gliding past. "He just left."

My heart aches for him and the burden left behind on shoulders too young to carry.

"And you haven't seen him since? Like ever?" I can't help asking.

"Nope. It's not like I haven't lived in the same house all my life."

"I get to see my dad on the weekends but sometimes he gets busy," Liam chimes in.

Chase nods once, jaw tight, eyes focused ahead.

There's heaviness in the air around us, and I wish I had arms long enough to wrap around both of them. Instead, I blurt out, "Favorite animal in three, two, one."

We all shout out our answers at the same time.

"Lion—"

"Penguin," Chase and I both shout simultaneously, our eyes snapping to each other before erupting into laughter.

"Penguins mate for life! You guys have to get married now!" Liam jumps up, bouncing on his toes.

Chase huffs out a quiet laugh. "Easy there, kid."

Ah, my cheeks burn. If I hear the word *marriage* one more time, I might actually scream. I shake my head and stand. "Why don't we get ready to head out? I need to stop at the store for curtains."

"Finally," Chase mutters, pushing off the bench.

The sound of his phone vibrating in his pocket cuts through the air. Like he's been doing all day, he pulls it out, barely glances at the screen, and sends the call straight to voicemail.

His face twists with annoyance, jaw clenched so tight I'm afraid his teeth might shatter.

I know without a doubt who it is.

Nora.

The only person who can steal Chase's peace.

7

CHASE

The noise of the zoo hums around us as the familiar buzz in my pocket sends a wave of irritation to instantly coil deep in my chest.

Tension shoots straight down my arm as I pull my phone out, squeezing it tight in my hand before sending the call to voicemail.

I don't even have to look at the number to know who's calling.

Izzy nudges my arm with her shoulder. "Why don't you just block her before you break your phone?"

"I don't know," I mutter, dragging my arm out from behind her and leaning forward onto my knees. I know I don't have a goddamn thing to say to Nora, but I can't seem to turn my back on her completely. I feel like I'm still that little kid, her Chasey-fucking-boy, always leaving the front door unlocked for her.

"So, then pick up the call and see what she wants," she urges, nudging her knee against mine.

I shake my head quietly. "I know what she wants. For me to

68

come down to whatever treatment facility she's at and bail her out. I'm not doing that again."

"You know you don't owe her anything," she says, reaching out to gently brush her fingers over the side of my hair. When it was longer, her hands would linger—tugging, twisting. Now, they don't have anything to catch on to, and she pulls away all too soon.

I can tell she misses my longer hair. It's only been a few days since I showed up at her apartment with clippers in hand.

"Are you sure about this?"

"For the millionth time, yes," I said, sitting on the closed lid of her toilet. "Just do it."

"This—" Izzy stood behind me, holding up the brand-new clippers I bought, her eyes meeting mine in the mirror, "—is not what I thought you meant when you said you needed a hand with something."

I huffed out a quiet laugh. "What did you think I meant?"

"Sex," she deadpanned. "I thought you meant sex, Chase."

A smile pulled at my mouth as I glanced at her reflection.

She was standing there in nothing but a T-shirt and a pair of cotton panties that barely covered the bottom half of her ass.

"Still can," I said, dragging my eyes back up to meet her gaze. "After."

She rolled her eyes, then sucked her teeth, trying to hide a hint of a smile before taking a step closer.

"You're sure?" she asked, her voice soft.

"Positive." I held her gaze in the mirror.

"Okay," she replied, threading her fingers through my hair one last time.

The low buzz of the clippers filled the small bathroom as she sucked in a deep breath.

My long hair was my way of hiding from the reflection in the mirror, hiding from the man who was supposed to take care of us—take care of me.

But just like I want to know and see all the pieces of Izzy— the good, the bad, the ugly— I want her to see mine.

To see me.

"But you do deserve to heal," she says gently. "And you'll never get to do that until you face your demons, babe."

Fuck. She sees all of me, even the parts I don't.

My knee bounces under my arm as I mutter, "I'm not ready." I meet her patient gaze. "I feel like I'm finally learning to swim. If I go back there, let her in, she'll drag me down and drown us both." My voice is heavy with the weight of it.

"Lucky for you, I float," Izzy says, a slow smile spreading across her face.

My heart melts at that—at her, at the way she makes it all feel a little less heavy.

A chuckle slips out of me as I glance away. I don't know what I did to earn this woman, but I'll be damned if I don't work like hell to keep her.

My eyes drag low over her, taking in my black-and-white flannel hanging open over her low-cut black top.

She looks so fucking *mine.*

I grin. "Is that so?" I lean into her, our lips just a breath apart.

"Why do you guys kiss so much?" Liam interrupts.

We jump back. He's standing in front of us, lips tinged blue.

"We don't kiss that much," Izzy says, standing and ruffling his hair. "You ready to get out of here?"

He nods, then as I push up from the bench, he launches himself into me, arms wrapping tight around my middle.

"Whoa there, Knuckles," I say, surprised.

"Thanks for making my sister so happy," he whispers.

His words hit me harder than I expect.

"The last guy was dog water," he adds, making me choke on air.

That's a new one.

After grabbing curtains from a home goods store, we swing by Izzy's mom's house, where I left my car parked the day before. I'll be heading back to my place for the night, letting her and Liam have some quality time together.

I swallow down the lump in my throat at the thought of going back home. Realization hits. I feel more at home with Izzy than I ever did there.

"Bye, Thor," Liam calls out as we exit Izzy's car.

"Good night, Knuckles," I say when we stop at the sidewalk. He pounds my fist, then runs up the stairs of the townhouse.

Izzy stops in front of me, rising onto her tiptoes to press a quick kiss to my lips. "I'm just going to pop in and check on every-one, then it's a couch campout movie night," she says.

"On a school night, Miss Izzy?" I tease before dropping a kiss on her nose.

"That boy can't hang after nine. I give him ten minutes before he passes out."

"I'll see you tomorrow?" I ask, gently swaying her side to side, trying not to come off as needy as I feel.

"Tomorrow's Monday—I've got work and Liam, until Mom gets back," she says. "But Tuesday he has karate with the boys. Leslie will pick him up after school."

"Tuesday, then. Meet you at the gym?"

"Deal."

I lean down, wrapping my arms around her before forcing myself to let go.

"I love you," she says, her voice barely above a whisper.

"I love you more."

"Crazy." She giggles.

"Just for you."

I watch her as she walks inside, turning to wave back at me before disappearing through the door. My gaze lingers there a second too long—on the house, on the life waiting for her inside. I can picture it easily. Alfonso and Aiden probably deep in some video game they have no business playing, Layla doom scrolling somewhere while Lydia's tucked into a corner, sketchbook in hand, completely in her own world. Leslie would be on her laptop, headset on, working through calls with that no-nonsense tone she has.

And then there's me—standing out here.

The quiet settles in almost immediately. I flex my hand at my side, already missing the way hers fits in mine, before reaching into my pocket and grabbing my keys. I start toward my car a few houses down. The farther I get, the colder it feels —like the warmth Izzy carries with her disappears the second she's gone.

Five minutes too soon, I'm back at my place, diving into housework I've neglected—laundry, dishes, sorting through the week's mail. Unfortunately, it doesn't take long before everything's done and I'm stepping out of the shower, getting ready for bed.

My phone lights up on the counter.

Missed call. Voicemail.

Nora.

I exhale, debating for a second... then press play. I told myself I wouldn't listen to her messages, but here I am, ever the fucking masochist. Her voice spills out and before I realize it, my feet drag me toward her bedroom.

"Chasey Boy...it's me... Um, I'm at Hope Haven. I thought maybe you could come down. Visitation is on Tuesday from one to four. I miss my sweet boy. I can't believe it's been this long since I've seen your face. Okay, I'll see you soon.

To replay this message, press one. To delete, press seven. To save, press nine. For more options, press zero."

I stare up at the ceiling, at the yellowing spot above me from years of Nora's cigarette smoke, and press seven.

My hands squeeze the phone in a vice-like grip, every ounce of anger I've swallowed when it comes to her rising up all at once.

The silence in this house is suffocating, especially after spending so much time with Izzy. She can't sit in a room without the TV or music playing. Suddenly, my phone buzzes in my hand, the screen lighting up.

Like an answered prayer, Izzy's face glows softly in the darkness.

I hold the phone over my face and answer the video call, a smile tugging easily at the corners of my lips as I stare back at her.

"Hi," she says.

Two letters. One word. Completely meaningless from anyone else—but from her, it lights something in me.

"I was just thinking about you," I say, leaving Nora's room and heading upstairs to mine.

"Obviously, I missed you more." She bites her bottom lip.

"I didn't want to interrupt your time with your brother. What happened to the sofa sleepover?" I ask as I fall back onto my bed, not bothering with the lights.

"Couch campout movie night was a bust. Poor kid fell asleep during the short car ride home, then fought for his life trying to keep his eyes open long enough to get ready for bed," she replies with a laugh.

"We did have a long day," I say.

"I know. I'm exhausted," she says, her eyes heavy.

"You still in the living room?"

"In my bed. The couch was way too soft and killing my back."

"So... what are you wearing?" I ask, needing the sweet distraction if I'm going to get through the night.

Her soft laugh fills my ear, breathy and warm, loosening the tension in me.

I move one hand behind me and hold the phone with the other, stretching my arm out above me, giving Izzy a full view of my bare chest, the camera cutting off at the V of my lower abs.

"Show me," I say.

"You miss me already, Thor?" she asks, her voice teasing as she shifts onto her side, her dark eyes shining bright as they lower down the screen.

"I miss you always," I confess, as if she didn't already know how badly I want her by my side all the fucking time. It's probably not healthy, and I know I need to settle the fuck down, but with her, I'm an addict chasing her touch, her voice, the way I feel when I'm with her.

"I want to see you, Izzy. Show me," I say, softer this time.

She shifts again, the phone tilting slightly above her. The neckline of her top pulls low before she fixes it.

"Mom's calling," she says, her voice still coming through the phone.

I release a heavy sigh. scrubbing a hand over my face. Not because it kills the mood—but because I'm not ready to let her go yet.

"Of course she is. You should answer that."

"I'll text you tomorrow," she responds before saying good night.

She disappears and my home screen pops back up. I drop my phone beside me as it buzzes again, with a new text.

Isadorrra: Don't forget to study for NASM.

A second later it buzzes again, and this time a picture fills the message box. My breath catches in my throat at the sight of her.

"Fuck," I breathe out as my eyes hungrily devour the image.

The phone, held out in front of her, partially hides her face as she lies on her stomach. Her long dark hair falling over one shoulder, the loose neckline of her shirt dipping just enough that I catch the top of her breasts, while her free hand grips the fabric between them.

Isadorrra: Good night ;p

I stare at the photo again. With no other choice, my mind fills in the gaps, conjuring the rest of her and the luscious bottom half she left out.

8

IZZY

"Hi, Ma," I say automatically. "Liam's already asleep."

I roll onto my back, phone pressed to my ear.

"Oh, okay." She sighs, the sound crackling over the phone.

I push up onto my elbow, listening more closely. There's rustling on her end, a zipper dragging, a loud thud like something was tossed instead of set down.

"What's wrong?" I ask.

"No, nothing," she says too quickly. "Nothing at all. I'm just packing."

My stomach drops. "What happened?"

She lets out a laugh—short, sharp, and wrong. Every alarm bell in my head goes off. This is bad.

"We didn't even make it through dinner," she says. "Fucking dinner!" she snaps.

I flinch, my brows pulling together. She never curses like that. Not with us.

A dozen questions sit on the tip of my tongue, but I swallow them down. "I'm so sorry, Mom."

"It's fine. I'm fine—" she cuts herself off with a sharp breath. "I just—I wanted to give you a heads up so you can bring Liam to the house tomorrow after school…"

Something zips loudly on her end.

"I got a flight out first thing in the morning," she blurts, her tone flat.

Like she's already moved past this.

Different man. Same ending.

My heart aches for her, knowing in the end all she really wants is a love that stays.

"Thank you for taking him, baby girl," she adds, like nothing just happened. "I'm sure he's been enjoying his Izzy time even if it's been cut short."

"Of course, Mom. You don't have to thank me for that. He can stay for the rest of the week if you need—"

"No," she cuts me off.

I press my lips together, swallowing the rest of my words. "Okay."

My grip tightens around my phone.

Whatever happened, she's not going to talk about it. Not right now.

As soon as I end the call with Mom, I'm swiping through my phone like a woman possessed, fresh tea sitting heavy on my tongue. I pull up my favorites. My thumb hovers over Mya's name before I force myself to scroll down and tap the very last name on the list instead.

"Yeah?" Leslie answers, her tone clipped.

"Why do you always answer the phone like that?" I mutter.

Like I'm a bother.

I don't know why I still expect it to feel different.

"I'm working, Izzy. What's up?"

"It's ten o'clock at night."

"And? I got promoted to a later shift," she says, a little edge creeping in.

I huff under my breath. "Since when is the graveyard shift a promotion?"

She exhales sharply. "Did you call me for a reason or just to talk shit?"

"Fine. Did Mom call you?"

"Nope."

Something inside me flickers. I bite the inside of my cheek, holding it in.

Mom had Leslie at fifteen. In a lot of ways, they grew up together—just the two of them, long before the rest of us showed up. Their bond has always been something I've envied, at least a little.

So yeah. This feels like a very small win—even if it's only because I'm the one with Liam.

"I can hear you thinking," she says. "What's going on?"

I shift onto my back. "She's cutting the honeymoon short. Coming back tomorrow."

"What? Why?"

"She wouldn't say." I stare up at the ceiling, my stomach twisting as I replay our conversation in my mind. "But you know how she gets."

"What the hell could've gone wrong in less than twenty-four hours?" Leslie asks, her voice growing quiet like she's in thought. "That woman doesn't stay where she doesn't feel right. Ever."

My chest tightens.

She's right.

But Mom and Luis have been good. Better than good. So, what the hell happened?

"You think she's going to bail?" I ask. "She was ready to move to Jersey yesterday. What could've—"

"Izzy."

I stop.

"Don't start spiraling," she says. "You know how she is."

I let out a breath, pressing my phone tighter to my ear.

"Yeah," I mumble. "I do."

The next morning, I'm kicking myself for spending an extra hour and a half on the phone with Mya after my call with Leslie. Desperate for the sweet relief of my morning coffee, I start the Keurig, waiting for it to warm up while responding to Chase's *'morning beautiful'* text. I grin like a fool at the message, practically hearing the timbre of his morning voice as if he were here saying it in person. I know, I know. We're definitely in too deep, and eventually these butterflies will fade over time along with these sweet messages. But for now, I'll cling to them for as long as I can.

I send a gif of Cam from Modern Family, crying in bed, with the caption, 'Why are Mondays so hard?'

His response is immediate.

Thor: More like, me last night after that text you sent.

I reply with an evil laughing emoji.

Thor: You won't be laughing when I get my hands on–and in–you.

Me: Promises, promises, Thor.

The next picture comes through.

Chase at the veterinary clinic he works at during the day as a vet tech. He's crouched on the floor in black scrubs, one knee down, a sleepy dog with floppy ears leaning into his side.

Thor: Been here since five-thirty for surgery prep. He's not impressed.

Thor: I'm here until four, then the gym for more training with Damon. How's your Mom and Luis doing?

Me: Not good. Mom is flying back in today, so I'm going straight to the house after school to see what's going on.

The dots on the screen bubble up and disappear, then reappear before his message comes through.

Thor: Is everything okay?

Me: No clue yet. I'll find out tonight.

As the rich aroma of coffee finally fills my small kitchen, barely separated from the living room by a tiny island, Liam pops his head up from the couch across from me.

"I fell asleep," he mumbles, scrambling up from the makeshift bed. His dark curls stick up in every direction as he stumbles over to me.

I chuckle, tousling his hair when he wraps his little arms around me. "It happens to all of us at least once a day every day, buddy."

"Can we finish the movie tonight?" Liam asks, giving me his best puppy-dog eyes.

"Actually, Mom is coming back today, so—"

"Why?" He rears back.

Definitely not the reaction I was expecting.

"She missed us."

Liam glares at me with a blank face. "Nope, that's not it."

"I don't know, but whatever it is, she'll get through it like she always does."

"Maybe she left Luis in Jamaica."

"Hey, what's that about?"

"Nothing, I'm going to get ready for school."

I stare after him, shaking my head as he heads to the bathroom, my mind spinning over how he has been acting lately. He's not even my child, and he's got me stressed.

"Your turn to pick a song bud," I say, reaching for my phone tethered into my car's auxiliary port. Liam has been in a less than ecstatic mood since I told him Mom was coming back today, and it was no better after school either. After confirming Mom got in a couple of hours ago, I decide to meet up with Mya at the playground first, –giving mom time to settle in before we head over.

The Old Town Road remix with Billy Ray Cyrus blasts through my speakers, the bass shaking my car and making Liam giggle. I can't help but smile in satisfaction at having cheered him up, even if just a little.

Mya waves at us, smiling as she stands on the sidewalk with baby Zion strapped to her chest in a carrier. I park in the spot in front of her and jump out of the car, making a beeline for Zion.

"Kid swap, please. This one doesn't talk back," I say immediately reaching for my Z bear. He squeals when he notices me, melting my heart.

"Race you down the slide," Mya tells Liam once she unwraps Zion and hands him to me. I watch them take off.

While they run around, I pop Zion into a baby swing and give him a soft push. He smiles wide, the nubs of two bottom teeth peeking through. His sweet, innocent joy is contagious as he giggles with each sway.

Mya finally makes her way over to us, one hand on her side as she tries to catch her breath. I reach out a hand, giving Zion's swing another gentle push as he lets out a soft giggle at the sight of his mama.

"Fudge," she huffs. "I tap out."

"Fudge? Are you hungry? I might have one of Chase's protein bars in the car," I respond, immediately reaching for my keys.

"No, I'm not hungry." She laughs. "I'm reading a new book about the energy words carry and how they lower our vibes. Trying not to bring unneeded negativity to my son with all the cussing. So, watch your mother fudging-mouth, bish."

I struggle to contain the laughter bursting at the seams of my mouth. "I'm sorry, who are you and what the fudge have you done with my best friend?"

"Leave me alone. You'll see when you and Daddy Thor are making little baby Avengers of your own," she says, gyrating her hips.

"Not Daddy Thor." I choke on air. "It's been a month. There will be no mini-Avengers running around over here for a long while."

"You guys are moving pretty fast, already declaring your undying love. I give it a few more weeks before you move in together. I mean, he's already there all the time anyway, and before you know it, he'll be dropping down on one knee."

Zion kicks his legs, letting out a happy squeal as the swing slows, and I nudge it again absentmindedly.

"You were also dead sure about—"

"No, ma'am, I sure was not," she cuts me off with a pointed finger in my direction. "Cara de culo was nothing but a leech from the very beginning, just stringing you along and using you for all he could. And we both know I told you that often. But you wanted him to be the one and I entertained your delulu because I love you and you deserve all the things you wish for in this life."

My lips turn down in a frown. "I love you," I say, dropping my arm over her shoulder, feeling so grateful for her loyalty.

"Love you too, Izzy boo. But mark my words, that man is crazy about you. I doubt he is going to waste much time before making you his forever and ever and ever," she teases, tickling my side. I laugh, swatting her hands away. Still, a moment later, something heavier settles in my chest.

My shoulders sink. "I don't know, Mya. I think something is wrong with me. No matter how much I want to believe in this, a part of me can't help waiting for it to fall apart."

"Hey," Mya wraps her arm around my shoulder. "Your heart is still healing and that is okay. You deserve this, Izzy boo."

I stare out at the playground for a second, chewing on the inside of my cheek as Liam, in front of us, fights gravity trying to climb up the slide.

I look at Mya. "I'm pretty sure Nora called him, like, thirty-seven times today."

"Isn't she in jail?"

"Court-ordered rehab."

"It's just been him dealing with her his whole life, right? Where is his dad?"

"He doesn't know." I shrug. "Said he walked out the door one day and never came back." A knot squeezes in my chest at the thought of a little Chase having to watch his father leave like that.

"So, let's find him!" Liam cuts in, his excitement lighting up his wide eyes as he pops up in front of me and Mya.

"Liam, what has mom told you about listening in on adult conversations?"

"But Izzy, maybe his dad just got lost or something. If we make signs and—"

"Slow down, buddy. This isn't like a lost pet." If only it were that simple.

"Well—" Mya shrugs. "I mean, I'm not a detective, but I am a realtor. I can pull property records. He grew up in that house, right? His dad might've been on the deed before he left."

"See, Izzy!" Liam blurts, tugging on my arm.

"No. You can't just go looking for people."

"Your sister's right, buddy. I don't know what I was thinking," Mya says, giving me an apologetic look.

"But why?" he asks, his small face scrunching, like he can't understand why we wouldn't try.

"Because..." I hesitate, searching for the best words that will help him understand while not crushing his spirit. "Sometimes people are complicated. And sometimes they don't want to be found."

"But he's his dad. Why would he just leave him alone?"

"Hey," I say gently, forcing a smile. "How about we go spin on the merry-go-round?"

"Oh no," Mya mutters behind me.

A second later, it hits me.

"Ew, what's that smell?" Liam cries, pinching his nose.

Mya grimaces, holding Zion at arm's length. "And that's our cue to get home."

She taps her cheek to mine. "I'll let you know what I can dig up," she whispers with a wink.

"Mya. No."

She waves me and Liam goodbye, taking Zion's little hand and lifting it in a wave.

I roll my eyes, but I don't argue again. I'd be lying if a part of me didn't want to know. I mean, I doubt she'll be able to find anything.

When we get to Mom's, Liam completely surprises me by jumping out of the car and racing up the stairs as soon as I put the car in park. I grab my bag and follow, pulling the front door closed behind me. The living room is dim. The lamp by the sofa casts a soft glow across the furniture but there's no other sign that anyone is here.

No TV. No music. No movement.

"Ma?"

"I'm in the kitchen," she calls back, her voice carrying, but lacking its usual warmth.

I follow the sound of her voice and find Mom, bent over Liam, in a tight embrace. Her arms wrap fully around him like she hasn't seen him in weeks instead of days. His sneakers barely touch the floor as she squeezes him close.

When she finally notices me, she straightens. She's already in pajamas, a gray robe cinched tightly at her waist, her short pixie hair tucked neatly under a satin bonnet. Her face is bare of makeup, not even the lipstick she wears every day. She looks more tired than I've ever seen her and nothing like the woman who was glowing at her wedding just a few days ago.

She crosses the kitchen in two quick steps and pulls me into her arms. The hug lingers a little longer than usual. I pull back slowly but keep hold of her fingers, squeezing until she finally looks up at me.

My eyes search hers.

"I'm good, mama," she says, dropping her gaze too fast. But I catch it anyway—the glassy look in her eyes and the puffiness underneath them.

She's been crying.

My heart squeezes tight.

"Did you bring back anything from Jamaica?" Liam asks, pulling our attention. His eyes are wide and completely oblivious to Mom.

"Of course I did. It's sitting on your bed."

Liam gasps, then bolts out of the kitchen, his steps thundering up the stairs.

"Shower right after!" she shouts, then looks at me. "And you get something, too." She holds up a coffee mug like she's trying to sell it to me.

"Cute," I say, thanking her, even though my attention stays fixed on her face—on the way she continues to avoid my gaze.

"Are you staying for dinner?" she asks.

"I don't know yet."

She turns back to the counter, fiddling with something I can't see. "It's pizza. Your sister should be back any minute with it."

My brows pull together. "You don't eat pizza."

"Well, today se me antojo," she says, a little too quickly. "And all your sister has in the fridge is those fresh meal kits."

She keeps moving through the kitchen, keeping her back to me, like if she stops for even a second, something might spill over.

The front door shuts with a loud thud, and Leslie's voice follows it in, barking at the boys to get upstairs and wash up.

She steps into the kitchen a second later, two boxes of pizza in her hands, her eyes instantly finding mine and then motioning with her lips toward mom. I frown, turning my eyes back to Mom as she grabs the step stool between the wall and fridge and places it in front of the stove so she can reach the cabinet above it.

My stomach twists.

"Cue the playlist," she whispers into my ear as Mom pulls out the emergency rum, reserved strictly for ailments of the heart. A chill crawls down my neck when my body recalls the last time we reached for that bottle...and how quickly it emptied.

Leslie drops the two pizza boxes in the center of the kitchen table, paper plates stacked on top, while Mom tips the Brugal into three mismatched Jamaica mugs, like this is just another normal night.

She places our mugs in front of us, mine a black and yellow one with the words *one love* and Leslie's a red, gold, and green one stamped with *Irie*.

"So, what happened? Leslie asks.

"What do you mean?" Mom says.

Leslie and I both share a look.

Is she serious right now?

"You're tapping into the Brugal on a Monday afternoon over pizza in the middle of your honeymoon."

Mom sucks her teeth, annoyed. "Since when did you two get so dramatic?" She won't look at either of us. I don't miss the way Leslie's eyes flick to me again, this time sharper.

"Ma..." I ask.

"Can't a mother just sit with her daughters and enjoy their company?"

We both raise our eyebrows.

"Mom," Leslie says slowly.

She sighs, wrapping both hands around her mug. "Nothing is wrong. Luis is fine. I'm fine. Pero ya se acabó el honeymoon."

Her fingers tighten around the mug.

She swallows.

"Everything was fine until we got to Jamaica and suddenly my swimsuit is 'too revealing', and everything I do is too much and he's accusing me of flirting with other men. By dinner, he's telling me I'm his wife now and should act accordingly," she says, letting out a short humorless laugh.

The kitchen door flies open.

"Pizza!" Aiden calls out as he, Liam, and his brother Alfonso barrel into the kitchen, socks sliding against the floor, shirts rumpled from the day, as they swarm the table before anyone can stop them.

Leslie immediately swoops in, lifting one of the pizza boxes over her head. "How about pizza in the living room?"

"Yes!" They shout together, turning around.

"Wait!" Mom calls out.

Leslie and the boys crowd the doorway while Mom scooches out of her chair and grabs the roll of paper towels on the counter.

She hands it to Leslie. "Not a stain on Mami's muebles."

Leslie takes it and they all walk out.

Mom settles back down into the dining table chair beside me. I watch her flip open the other pizza box, grab a slice, and sink into it like she's hoping it will fill more than her stomach.

Leslie reappears in the doorway a second later, the boys' voices muffled from the living room behind her. She grabs her mug off the counter, taking a slow sip like, she's bracing herself.

"Okay," she says, leaning back against the counter. "Start from the top. What actually happened?"

Mom exhales through her nose.

"He got jealous," she says flatly.

Leslie's brows lift. "Of what?"

"Of me existing," Mom snaps. "Of me talking, laughing— breathing, probably." She gestures vaguely. "I can't explain it, okay? He never acted like that before."

Leslie lets out a short breath, shaking her head as she takes another sip. "Some men get real comfortable once there's a ring on your finger."

"Exactly," Mom mutters.

I wrap my hands around my mug, the warmth grounding me even as my chest tightens.

"He knew what he was getting into when he asked you to marry him," I say carefully.

Mom huffs. "Yeah. Before I was his wife."

Silence.

Leslie's expression shifts—something sharper, more knowing.

"Ah," she mutters. "There it is."

Mom points at her. "Don't start."

"I'm not starting," Leslie says, pushing off the counter. "I'm just saying—some men hear 'wife' and suddenly think it means ownership."

Mom scoffs, but there's no real bite behind it this time. "Well, he picked the wrong one."

"Clearly."

I glance between them, something uneasy settling in my chest.

"And now?" Leslie asks, quieter.

Mom's shoulders drop just slightly. "Now I'm trying to figure out if I can do this long-term." She looks down at her mug. "Because this isn't a one-time thing. This is who he is."

The words hang heavy.

"And I don't know if I'm okay with that being my life too."

Leslie doesn't respond right away.

She just takes another slow sip.

Thinking.

That's what she does—she doesn't react, she assesses.

"When something doesn't feel right..." I start.

"I don't stay," Mom finishes.

Leslie nods once, like that tracks.

Like it always has.

Different man. Same ending.

My throat tightens.

"But you love him," I say softly.

Mom nods. "I do."

Leslie's gaze flicks to me, then back to Mom.

"Love's not the issue. It never is," Mom says quietly.

That lands harder than anything else.

Because she's not wrong.

Mom lets out a quiet laugh, wiping at her eyes. "I really thought this one would be different."

I reach for her hand without thinking, squeezing gently.

My heart aches for her, knowing in the end all she really wants is love.

"I'm so sorry, Ma."

She waves me off with one hand, but the other tightens around my own. "I'll figure it out. I always do."

And that's the part that scares me. Not that she left. But how easy it was. How quickly something good can change. Turn into something else entirely.

I stare down at my drink, the amber liquid catching the light. Because I can't stop thinking about it. About Chase. About us. About how good it feels right now.

And how fast that could change.

I take a sip, letting the burn settle in my chest.

Then I shove the thought down.

Hard.

Like if I don't look at it, it can't touch me.

9

CHASE

y muscles ache with the strain of the heavy weights, but I welcome the sweet burn, savoring it as sweat beads on my forehead and trickles down the sides of my face. Sucking in a deep breath, I lift the barbell into the air, the suspended weight pressing against my biceps and engaging the muscles in my shoulders, upper back, and abs. With a shaky exhale, I lower it, repeating the pattern again and again, getting lost in the familiar rhythm my body knows by heart. Pushing until there's nothing left to push through.

My phone buzzes on the floor and distracts me from the slow torment I'm currently inflicting on myself. It's been a busy couple of days, and Izzy has been pretty caught up with Liam and work, so we haven't spent much time together. Which may be for the better with the sour mood I've been in. Nora's calls have hijacked my phone. She's like a goddamn nightmare I'll never escape from. Her voicemails have gone from *sweet Chasey boy* to straight up volatile.

Raising the barbell one last time, I drop it on its holder and pull myself up. Catching my breath, I grab the towel hanging from my pocket and wipe the sweat off my face. It's pretty dead here for a Thursday night, but a few stragglers are as lost in their workouts as I just was. Suddenly, soft hands cover my eyes.

"Gotcha," Izzy whispers in my ear.

A smile tugs at the corners of my lips when I cover her hands with mine and pry them away from my face. I turn around, swinging my other leg over the bench to trap her between my legs. My hands glide over the soft material of her biker shorts.

"You've had me from the moment you landed in my arms, Izzy. You know that." I draw her closer with a gentle pull. "I missed you," I whisper. She lowers her face to mine, her dark hair creating a curtain around us as our lips meet in a kiss.

"I missed you. Sorry I've been M.I.A.," she says, her voice soft but not quite reaching her eyes.

"How's everything with your mom?" I ask, recalling our brief conversation about Lulu's return and Luis' emergency.

"Figuring things out."

"They'll be fine."

"You don't know my mom when she gets like this."

I frown. "Like what?"

"She starts looking for reasons it won't work. And then she decides she's done before it even has the chance to begin."

I take a step closer, a small smile pulling at my mouth. "But I know what it looks like when a man is in love. And Luis? He's too far gone to let her slip through his fingers."

Her brows lift. "Oh, yeah?"

"Ask me how I know," I mutter.

I slide my hands up and down her sides, the smooth stretch of her biker shorts beneath my palm. My thumbs graze the curve of her waist before my palms settle over the soft fullness of her hips. She fits there so easily, like she always does.

"How do you know?" she breathes against my lips, her fingers curling lightly into my shirt.

I smile, brushing my nose lightly against hers. "Because I know what it feels like to not want to be anywhere you're not."

Her lips curve and that's all the invitation I need. I close the distance and kiss her, lingering, letting myself have her for a second longer before pulling back just enough to look at her. I wrap an arm around her waist as I rise, lifting her in my arms. Her surprised squeal echoes softly through the gym.

"What are you—" she starts, but the rest of it dissolves into laughter as I haul her over my shoulder, one arm secure around her waist as she settles against me. "Chase!" She laughs, her hands gripping the back of my shirt as I start walking.

We make it a few steps before Damon catches us, "Hey—no manhandling the clients!" he calls out, already grinning.

I roll my eyes and lower her down anyway.

"I liked you better when you weren't my boss," I shoot back, flipping him off when he walks by with a stack of clean towels balanced against his hip.

He knocks my hand down in passing and leans in just long enough to give Izzy a quick side hug.

"Hey, Damon," she says, smoothing her hair back into place.

He shakes his head. "You two are something else. Keep it up though, happy looks good on him," he comments, punching my arm before walking off.

"Uh-oh," she says once he disappears around the corner, brows lifting. "Does that mean you've been going full *Ragnarok* in here?"

"I don't even know what that means," I chuckle, shaking my head. I avoid her eyes because I absolutely do know—thanks to the Avengers marathon she and Liam insisted on.

I reach for my pocket out of habit and come up empty. "Hold on." I glance back toward the free weights across the gym, spotting my phone still sitting on the bench.

"Be right back," I say, already jogging toward the racks.

I grab my water bottle and my phone from the weights and head back towards Izzy, then make the mistake of looking down at my screen.

My stomach drops at the string of missed calls and voicemails waiting at the top.

"Is she still calling?"

I glance up, realizing too late she's close enough to read everything on my face. For a second, I consider brushing it off. Instead, I turn the phone toward her and hit play on the last voicemail.

"You're a piece of shit. Just like your father!"

A sharp inhale sounds through the phone, followed by something clattering in the background.

"You think you're better than me now? Too good to answer your own mother's calls?"

Silence. Heavy breathing.

"Fuck you, Keagan. You're just like your piece of shit father. I didn't need him and I don't need you."

Another pause. Her voice shifts, smaller. Slurred.

"Chasey... baby, I didn't mean that."

Sniffling.

"I just need you to come get me. I can't stay here anymore. Nobody cares if I'm okay. You're the only one who ever does."

A shaky breath.

"Please don't leave me here."

The voicemail cuts off.

Izzy's hand settles against my arm—warm, steady. And for a second, it's enough to quiet everything else.

"I'm sorry, Chase. I hate that she keeps putting you in this position."

I nod once, jaw tight.

She's quiet for a second. "Have you ever thought about reaching out to your dad?"

The words hit wrong—too close, too exposed—and I react before I can stop myself.

"I don't need anything from him," I snap respond sharply.

But I did once. Years ago—when I wanted out. Out of this life. Out of being Nora's son.

I thought if I found him, he could help. The least he could do. It led nowhere. If he wanted to be found, he would've walked back in through the same door he left.

Her shoulders dip. "It was just a thought."

I drag a hand over my face, the edge in my voice dulling as fast as it came. "He'd just be another disappointment. And I'm already at capacity, Izzy."

"Maybe—" she starts, but I cut her off, needing a distraction.

"Feel like doing a circuit?" I interrupt, arching a brow at her.

Her face twists. "Who ever 'feels' like doing a circuit? Might as well 'feel' like dying," she responds, tilting her head to the side.

"I'll take it easy on you, promise."

"Weren't you just working out? Maybe you should rest or sit in the sauna for a little."

I shake my head knowing that I won't sit still long enough to actually rest. "I was just getting started," I lie, hating myself as soon as the words are out. "I'll keep it light."

She narrows her eyes at me. "Just listen to your body, okay?"

My head tilts to the side. "Who's the trainer in progress here?"

"Well, I do have an excellent trainer who reminds me of these things," she says, flashing a playful grin before we walk into the circuit area.

I set the timer on my watch for thirty minutes. Izzy automatically starts with some light stretches. Her movements are effortless, her form more confident than when we first started working out together.

My eyes linger longer than they should as she dips and twists. Everything in me quiets watching her, the way she settles into herself.

I drag a hand down the back of my neck, forcing myself to look away before I get stuck there.

I focus on prepping the circuit area instead, pulling out the kettlebells, dumbbells, and resistance bands we'll use, arranging the plyometric boxes at various heights.

Sixteen minutes in, my muscles are already quaking.

My brain tells me to stop but my body powers through the circuit, anyway. Sweat drips down my forehead and into my eyes. The tight strain builds in my muscles as each repetition gets harder and harder.

I stare down at the Plyometric box in front of me. *Just one more,* I tell myself. I inhale sharply as I glance at Izzy beside me. She's halfway through her own set and jumping up onto her shorter box.

I drop into a squat, steadying myself as best I can, gathering all the frustration simmering under my skin.

I suck in a breath and explode upward. The second I land, pain shoots through my leg. My balance slips—and I stumble back, clutching my thigh as it pulses with strain.

"Chase!" Izzy's voice cuts through the pounding in my ears, concern flashing across her face.

Grimacing, I grit my teeth and push up onto my elbows. She reaches for me. I grab her hand and haul myself up, but pain shoots through my leg, knocking the breath from my chest.

"Did you pull something?"

"Feels like it," I huff out, still catching my breath.

"You promised you would take it easy."

"I know!" I raise my voice, more due to the pain I'm in rather than anger. Izzy jolts, shoulders jumping to her ears as she stares at me wide-eyed.

Fuck.

"I'm sorry. I —" I clamp my jaw tight as another wave of pain engulfs my leg. Squeezing my hand into a tight ball, I bite down on it, unable to move.

"If it hurts this bad, you need a doctor, Chase," she says, a frown pulling at her lips.

I shake my head immediately. "Nothing's broken. I just need to get off it."

She slips under my arm to steady me just as Damon jogs over, brows pulled together as his gaze flicks from me to Izzy.

"What'd you do?" he asks.

"Pulled something," I grunt. "Muscle, probably."

Damon crouches, already reaching for my leg. "Let me see."

I shift back before he can touch it. "I'm good."

He straightens, unimpressed. "You're limping."

"Yeah," I mutter. "Because it hurts."

Damon hooks a hand under my other arm, steering me toward the front desk anyway. "Sit down before you make it worse."

I plant my good foot down, halting him from dragging me toward the front desk, and pull the opposite direction. "I just need to lie down!" The words come out sharper than I mean them to. Heat crawls up my neck. Half the gym's probably watching.

"Chase—" Damon starts.

"I'm fine," I insist, already angling us toward the exit.

"I left my car at home and jogged here," I add, like that somehow explains everything.

Izzy sighs. "Of course you did." She adjusts her grip under my arm. "I'll drive you."

Damon studies me for another second, clearly unconvinced, before relenting with a shake of his head. "Text me when you get home."

With Damon's help, we make it out to Izzy's car.

The drive is quiet. Izzy keeps her eyes on the road, and I want, badly, to reach for her hand, to hold onto the comfort she brings. But I'm too fucked up to try.

When we get to my place, she insists on taking me upstairs, but I convince her to leave me on the couch instead.

She disappears upstairs without another word and comes back a minute later with my phone charger and a couple of pillows. She slides one under my leg and another behind my head before heading into the kitchen.

When she returns, she's carrying Tylenol, a frozen bag of vegetables, and a glass of water.

"Thank you," I mutter before swallowing the tablets.

She lingers in front of me, her brows pulled tight, her bottom lip caught between her teeth like she's trying not to say something.

"I'm okay, Izzy. The pain has gone down already."

She shakes her head, her fingers twisting together at her sides. "I have to tell you something." She exhales, like she's bracing herself. Her eyes flick from my leg, then back to my face.

And there it is.

I brace myself for the words I know she is about to say. Words I am not ready to hear but I guess always knew would come. I lean onto my knees. The pain in my calf radiating as I try to focus on the words that I know without a doubt will break me and change me for the rest of my life. But at least we had these few months. At least I got a taste of sunlight before—

"A few days ago, I got it in my head to try and find your dad," she says, her voice tight. "Mya helped. She has access to property records through work and we plugged your address in and she started digging. It took her a while but...she found him." Her voice falters. "I know I should have talked to you first, but I just wanted to confirm it was him. He wants to see you."

I sit there, stilled by shock, staring at the woman I'm so hopelessly in love with as her words replay in my head again and again until they finally make sense. And even then, they don't. No, not at all what I was expecting. Yet, somehow, so much worse.

"Why?" My voice comes out foreign, rough.

"Because I see you," she says, her voice shaking. "I see what you've had to carry–your mom, him... all of it. And you're still standing."

I can't look at her. I squeeze my eyes shut for a second, like that might block it out.

"You didn't let it break you. But that doesn't mean you didn't deserve more. It doesn't mean he gets to just disappear like you never existed." Her eyes lock onto mine. "And I'm looking at you right now, Chase... and I can see how much of this you're still carrying. Still avoiding."

I nod my head but it doesn't feel real.

The room blurs. Izzy standing in front of me, her mouth moving–still talking–but her voice slips, like my brain can't hold onto her and what she just said at the same time. I don't realize I'm on my feet until I'm already moving, dragging myself up the stairs like my legs are wading through thick fog.

A part of me knows why she did it. She loves me and wants me whole. But the other part of me —

The louder part —

It feels like she took something I buried on purpose and dragged it back into the light.

She found him.

After all these years of me not looking—not wanting to look—she just... did it.

My jaw tightens.

I didn't ask for that.

"Chase."

I put more distance than I ever thought I would want between us and slam my bedroom door shut. The sound echoes through the empty house, a stark contrast to the turmoil inside of me. I pace back and forth, the pain in my leg a constant reminder of my physical limits, but the ache in my chest is something else entirely.

Pressure tightens in my chest–too many things at once. Shock. Anger. Betrayal. Something sharper I don't even have a name for.

Minutes pass, or maybe hours. I don't know.

Sitting on the edge of my bed, I finally hear a soft knock on the door. I don't respond. Another knock, firmer this time, followed by the sound of the door slowly creaking open.

"Can we talk about this, please?"

I drag a hand down my face, exhaling through my nose. I tip my head back and stare up at the ceiling because I can't face her right now.

"Talk about what, Izzy? How you went behind my back? How you thought it was okay to make decisions about my life without asking me?"

"I did it because I care about you." Her voice wavers. "Because I love you."

My eyes meet hers before I can stop myself.

Her wide eyes search mine, shining under the dim light. *Her.* She looks at me like that's supposed to fix it–like if I just believe her hard enough, it will undo what she did.

And fuck.

That almost hurts worse.

"You don't think I know that? But this—" I gesture wildly, trying to find the right words. "This is too much. You crossed a line."

"I know I did, and I'm sorry. But Chase, you deserve a chance to confront your past. To face your father."

"You have no idea what I deserve." I push to my feet too fast, my injured leg protesting immediately. A sharp pull shoots up my calf—but I don't stop until I'm standing and pacing the room.

"You have no idea what it's like to carry this weight around every day." My mom, my father, the life I never got to have because of them.

"No, I don't, but—"

"You can't just fix me!" The words come out harsher than I mean, echoing off the walls. Izzy flinches. Her shoulders pull in, fingers curling into themselves like she's trying to hold it together.

And I see it.

I see what I did.

But it's already out there.

I drag in a breath, but it doesn't help.

I sink back down onto the edge of the bed, slower this time, my leg forcing me to feel every inch of it. My hands brace against my thighs, head hanging for a second as everything crashes down at once.

"That's not what I'm trying to do," she says quietly.

I look up.

She hasn't moved.

Still standing near the door, like she doesn't know if she's allowed to come closer.

Her eyes are glassy now, bottom lip trembling just slightly, like she's fighting it. Fighting tears. Fighting me.

"Isn't it?" I shoot back, but there's less heat in it now. More exhaustion than anything. "You should leave."

The second I say it, I regret it. But I can't take it back?

"What?" Her voice breaks.

That— that almost does me in.

My fingers curl into the comforter. Say something. Fix it.

I don't.

Her face falls completely now. Not just hurt—heartbroken. Like I reached inside her chest and twisted something.

She searches my face one last time.

Waiting.

Hoping.

I don't give her anything.

"If that's what you really want," she whispers, her voice unsteady.

It's not.

What I want is to pretend the last thirty minutes never happened. What I want is for her to stay.

But all I do is sit there, watching as she turns to leave.

My eyes follow the line of her shoulder, the slight shake in her hands, the way she pauses at the door, just for a second, like she might turn back.

She doesn't.

The door clicks shut, soft. Final.

The silence engulfs me immediately, closing in on me from all sides like a heavy weight, and suddenly, I'm six years old again, standing on the porch, barely tall enough to see over the railing.

My small fingers clutch the frayed edge of my favorite stuffed animal, a worn Elmo with a missing eye. My father closes the trunk of his car with a heavy thud.

"Daddy, I want to go, too," I beg him, holding back tears in my eyes. He crouches down to my level, his tired gaze meeting mine.

"Be back before you know it, my boy. Just be a good boy for Mommy, okay?" His voice is soft.

I nod my head eagerly. "I'll be the best boy ever."

"I know you will."

"Keagan?" I hear Mom's sleepy voice calling father from inside. My father stares at the open door behind me, both of us knowing he's the Keagan she's calling for. Instead of going to her, he takes a step back. Then he walks out the door.

Just like Izzy does.

10

———

IZZY

My heart aches with each step I take away from his bedroom door, the pain in his words echoing in my mind. I know giving him space to battle the demons haunting him are the logical choice and what he needs most. But my heart, already tethered to his, begs me to turn around.

My doubts and insecurities are louder, though.

They creep in, merciless and familiar, like they've been waiting for this exact moment.

They swirl in my mind, whispering their poison as the door clicks shut behind me.

You crossed the line.

I might have just ruined this.

I bite down on my bottom lip, the fear of losing him washing over me, as well as the certainty that I already have.

The night air hits my face the second the door shuts behind me, cool against my flushed skin. I walk down the steps, toward my parked car, and further away from Chase. A heavy knot coils around my insides, squeezing me like a vice. By the time I slide into my driver's seat, my vision is blurred with tears.

Seatbelt. Ignition. Drive.

I don't call Mya to talk me off the ledge or even play music, my usual refuge to distract me. No, I keep my eyes forward on the drive home and let the silence swallow me whole as the image of him pacing his bedroom flashes in my mind. The look on his face when I told him the truth. The way something inside him seemed to break.

What was I thinking?

It isn't long before the sight of Mom's house comes to view, its warm lights glowing downstairs. Like a beacon, it calls out to me, urging me to stop and seek refuge within those walls. But the heaviness in my chest keeps me rooted in place, dragging me back to the last time I stood on her front step, ashamed and heartbroken.

The night my last relationship fell apart, leaving me shattered.

And now here I am again.

Last time, I didn't see it coming,

This time...

I know exactly what I did.

A small, humorless laugh slips out of me.

This is what I get for throwing caution to the wind. For letting myself fall.

And for ultimately being the one to wreck us.

I swipe at my cheeks with the heel of my hand and press harder on the gas, driving past without slowing.

Guilt, regret, and something heavier settle deep in my chest, pushing me forward—toward an empty apartment I'm not ready to sit in.

"I fucked up, Mya," I say, placing the phone on my chest so I can use both hands to hold up the carton of rum raisin ice cream currently sweating beads of frost on my lap.

"Yeah, you kind of did, but you were coming from a place of love," Mya says through my phone speaker.

"He hates me," I mutter, taking a large spoonful into my mouth.

"Probably," she grumbles without hesitation.

"Mya!" I cry out, the sound escaping me as a sharp jolt of pain pierces through my skull. I put the spoon back in the pint carton.

"I'm not sugarcoating this. You said you were going to sit on this information and instead you dropped a nuclear bomb after your man pulled a muscle in his leg while he was trying to outrun his feelings."

"I know, I know," I whisper. "I didn't mean to drop it on him like that," I add quickly. "But after hearing the voicemail his mom left him...seeing how much she still affects him, I couldn't keep it to myself. I thought if maybe at least one adult in his life apologized...it might give him some closure."

"You decided what healing looks like for him."

I shove another spoonful in my mouth, barely tasting it, and let out a frustrated sigh, dropping my head back against the sofa. I stare up at the ceiling. "I ruined everything."

"You can't fight battles he hasn't chosen to face."

I squeeze my eyes shut.

"I know, Mya. It's just..." The pressure in my chest squeezes tight, cutting off the rest of my words and making it hard to breathe. I can't escape the wave of sadness that engulfs me as our time together flashes in my mind. Is this the end? We barely even started. "Love isn't supposed to feel like this."

"What? Scary as fuck? Get your head out of your Disney princess fantasy, Izzy. Love is not some shining white knight whose got his shit together, coming to save you. Sometimes it's messy, scary, and completely at odds with where you thought life was supposed to take you. Do you not remember when Kev and I first started dating?"

A small smile pulls at my lips. "When you were convinced he was love bombing you?"

We both laugh at that, remembering her panic and confusion over his pure intentions.

"Yes. I was so caught up in my fears that I could have missed out on all of this, Izzy. If I hadn't taken that chance on this man—on what could be—I wouldn't have learned what he's taught me about trust and vulnerability. Love is not perfect, but for the right person, it's absolutely worth navigating the chaos for."

"Okay, but you had serious commitment issues back then."

"And you don't?" Mya's voice rises. "Cara de culo ran a number on you, boo. But yes, before Kev, I definitely scared every man out of my life; however, no matter what I threw at him, he responded with patience and acceptance. He made me really reevaluate the past trauma. I was unknowingly projecting onto him."

"So, I'm the problem. It's me."

"No, Taylor Swift," she deadpans. "Sit down. I'm just saying it's not up to you to fix him or his trauma. And again, you said you were going to wait and instead you went right ahead and reached out to the man that abandoned him."

"I wasn't trying to fix him." My voice cracks. "I'm not. I just—" I exhale, shaking my head. "I don't know how I got here. How I let this happen again."

"This is not the same thing as you and what's-his-face."

"Well, it hurts just as much," I say, my chest aching in a way I can't shake. "Actually, no, no, it isn't the same. Back then, it felt like the ground got ripped out from under me." I let out a shaky breath. "This... this is worse. Because I'm the one who did the damage."

"Do you hear yourself right now?" She says, quieter now. "You already know this isn't the same. So don't turn it into something it's not. You messed up—yeah. That doesn't have to mean it's over."

Her words sink in deep, like pressing against a wound that's still tender, because she's right.

The spiral in my head slowing just enough to hear it.

"I just...don't know how to fix it."

"I'm over your pity party," she announces. "Z fell asleep for the night, and if I pump now, I can dump the next batch. Do you want to drown your sorrows in wine or rum?"

My mind instantly flashes to my most recent hangover and Chase taking care of me. "Bring whatever you want." I sigh. "You'll have to drown yourself in sorrows for the both of us."

"Oh boy," she mutters, laughing at me under her breath. "I'll see you in a few."

I push myself off the couch when the line goes dead and I reluctantly return the half-empty carton of ice cream to the freezer. Settling back into my spot on the couch, I try to distract myself from the gaping hole in my chest by absentmindedly scrolling through social media while I wait for Mya.

Before I can stop myself, I'm tapping Chase's name, typing *I'm sorry* into the message bar.

The words stare back at me from the screen, small and useless. My thumb hovers over the send button before deleting them altogether. Those two little words can't undo the hurt I caused him.

But walking away won't either.

So, instead, I brace myself and press the call button.

11

———

CHASE

"Hey, it's me," Izzy says with a sigh. Her voice sounds softer than usual, like she let out a breath before speaking. "I really hoped you'd pick up but I guess not..." I can almost see the slight crease forming between her brows, her lips pressing together the way they do when she's worried.

"Look, about tonight... I just want you to know I'm really sorry, Chase. I should have respected your feelings about your dad. It was wrong of me to reach out without talking to you first." Her voice trembles, and my chest tightens. "I know there's no excuse for what I did. I crossed a line, and I'm so sorry. I care about you so much... and hearing those voicemails—seeing how much of that you still carry—I couldn't just sit there and do nothing. I thought if I could help fix even a piece of it for you, I should. But that wasn't my call to make. I see that now." Her voice softens. "I just hope we can move forward from here... whether that's together or as friends. I'm here when you're ready."

"To replay this message, press one. To delete—"

I press my finger against the bright screen of my phone, replaying the message for the third time before dropping it onto

116

my chest. My heavy breathing fills the air as I try to control the anger swirling inside of me from her words. Then her soft voice breaks through the dark void around me again.

How fast everything went to shit guts me. I wish I could've handled it better. I wish she were here instead of miles away, apologizing in my arms instead of my voicemail. But my brain won't let me stay in that version of it, though—it keeps dragging me back to the fact that this woman I'm in love with did in fact go behind my back to contact the man who abandoned me.

The last part of her message replays—the 'or friends' part instantly making me tense, my jaw locking like if I listen hard enough the words might change. I hate that we're here. Like this. I hate that she's doubting us right now, and that same doubt has seeped its way through the phone line and into the cracks of my heart. My heart, which suddenly couldn't give a damn about my parental issues, drops when she's talking about us being friends. I don't know if I can forgive her right now, but I do know I can never just be her goddamn friend.

I sit up and take a deep breath, dropping my elbows to my knees and cradling my phone in my hands. I debate whether to call or text her back. My phone buzzes with an incoming text.

Isadorra: I'm here whenever you're ready.

I read the message but hear her voice echoing in my mind. It's as if she's standing right in front of me, waiting for an answer I'm not sure I can give. My heart races, caught between wanting to reach out and the fear of what comes after tonight.

My thumb hovers over the screen. The weight of my whole life presses down on me. I'm stuck in the middle of my fucked up past and the future I could have with Izzy.

I toss my phone onto the bed and stand.

Pain grips my leg, sharp enough to make me suck in a breath—a reminder of the idiot I was earlier.

I drop back onto the mattress.

Stuck here all over again.

After a while of staring into the dark, a faint knock comes from downstairs. I freeze, focusing on every creak of this old house when I hear it again. A sudden rush of hope washes over me, my mind quickly picturing Izzy on the other side.

She came back.

Ignoring the sharp pain in my leg, I rush out of the bedroom, limping as fast as I can down the stairs. The light from the living room spills into the hallway, stinging my eyes after so long in the dark. I squint toward the door, my heart racing as I shove every doubt aside. I just need to see her. To make this right— and most importantly, fuck that "we can be friends" shit.

I swing the door open, my eyes dropping to where Izzy's face should be, only to find myself staring at the solid chest of a man. When I look up, piercing green eyes meet mine, cold and shocking as a bucket of ice water.

"Son."

I'm imagining this. I have to be. But the longer I stare, the harder it is to deny it. He looks like I remember—just older. More worn. Same height as me. Same blond hair, now streaked with gray. Green eyes stare back at me like I'm the one out of place. Same sharp jaw, like time didn't soften it—just carved deeper into it.

My stomach drops. I feel nauseous.

I must be imagining this, because there's no way the man who walked out on me all those years ago is standing here like this.

Like he belongs here. Like he gets to come back.

"Nope." I slam the door shut and limp back toward the stairs.

I make it up the first few steps before the pain pulsing through my leg is too much. I stop and sink into the steps as my body shakes. This is what I get for getting my hopes up and running down the stairs.

The knocking comes again. I shake my head in disbelief.

"This can't be happening," I mutter to myself.

The door creaks open.

I don't turn around. I don't need to.

I barely hear the sound of his footfalls over the years worth of pent-up anger bubble up inside of me.

The nerve of this guy. Almost twenty years and now he chooses to walk through that door like he never even left. Tonight of all nights.

"Walk right in, why don't you?" I scoff.

"K.C.," he says, stopping in front of me.

I grit my teeth at the nickname I haven't heard in ages. It hits somewhere deeper than I expect—sharp and unwelcome. "Don't call me that." My words come out clipped and sharp. My hands tremble at my sides. I ball them into tight fists as if squeezing them tighter will keep the storm inside from bursting through.

Keagan sighs, bringing his hands to his sides. "Your little girl-friend, Izzy, called. Real sweet—"

"Don't," I cut him off, squeezing my eyes shut as the last bit of my resolve starts to crumble at the mere mention of Izzy's name. The mother-fucking nerve. "You don't speak her name."

I open my eyes and rise to my feet, glaring at him. Squaring my shoulders back, I've easily got a couple of inches on him, but seeing him, exactly as I remember, in grease-stained jeans and an oversized flannel, I transport to that six-year-old all over again.

Heat rushes through my skin, setting every nerve on fire, and I'm helpless to the memories flooding in. The years wasted staring out that door, wishing for him to come back. To take me with him. Away from here. Away from Nora? Every birthday he missed. Every school function Nora was too fucked up to show up for. Every day I had to sit there and take care of her because no one else was there to do it.

I'm not the one who left. I wasn't the one who was supposed to go chasing after him.

Not when all he had to do was walk back through that door. Come back home.

My heart pounds in my chest, a relentless reminder of the anger I've tried to bury—just like he clearly buried the memory of me.

How dare he show up here now. Only after Izzy called him.

"You don't get to come in here like it's any other day," I say through clenched teeth, barely holding back my rage.

He takes a few steps forward, his eyes searching mine. What does he see? All Nora ever saw was him in me. When I look in the mirror, I see the boy still stuck here picking up the pieces he left behind. "You think this is easy for me? I've tried reaching out to you a million times."

"Easy?" The word sends a chill straight through me, my vision blurring. I close the distance between us until I'm in his face. "Do you really think it's been easy for me? I was just a kid and you left me! Alone! With her!"

He doesn't flinch. Instead he looks away, his eyes shining with unshed tears. My own chest heaves frantically as I force my own tears back. I wasted too many of them on him the day he left. I won't let another fall.

"I did that," he admits, his voice thick with regret. "I'm sorry, son. I thought–I thought if I left for good things would be better. Your mother—"

Before I can process my body's reaction, the anger I've been struggling to contain spills over. My arm swings through the air, my fist connecting with the side of his face. The impact ricochets through my bones, striking straight to my gut. He stumbles back, crashing against the wall, momentarily stunned.

I don't feel any better, but I'm consumed by this rage, overflowing with a lifetime of things I've needed to say to him. "Better for who?" I shout as he drags himself up. "I was six years old! And the mother you left me with is fucking crazy, but you thought leaving the kid behind would magically fix her, right? God, you have no idea what I've had to endure—all because you were too fucking selfish. You've thought of no one but yourself that day and every damn day since!" The veins in my neck throb with the force of my words.

He stands there rubbing his jaw like he's contemplating mine or his next move. "You done?"

The heaviness I've carried inside of me for so long is desperate to get it all out once and for all, but for what? I wish throwing that punch had felt more satisfying; instead, I feel pretty fucking empty right now. "I'm barely getting started, but I'm done wasting another minute in the past," I say, turning to head back upstairs.

"I agree," he calls back.

"Great." I don't bother turning around and place one hand on the banister of the stairs. "I'm sure you remember your way out."

I take the first step up the stairs, the weight of my leg growing heavy as I drag it up.

"Wait," he calls out. I pause, unable to really put up much of a fight. I'm beyond exhausted, emotionally and physically. I lean against the banister for support, relieving the burning pain in my leg. It might just fall off. "Just hold on, please. You don't owe me nothing and I know you weren't just going to forgive me at the mere sight of me, okay? But I'm not asking to pick up from where we left off and be best friends. I will never forgive myself for leaving you, son. I have to live and die with that. So, if you want to hit me, go ahead. I deserve it and more, but it's taken me almost twenty years to get here. I'm not just going to walk back out that door."

I take a deep breath, gripping the banister as I search his face for any hint of what his true motive might be. "Why? Why now after all this time? Where have you even been?"

"Can we please sit? I'm gonna get a crick in my neck from trying to stare up at you... Geeze, I wasn't expecting you to be so—" He waves his hand in front of me, searching for the right words before giving up, scratching the back of his head and chuckling nervously to himself.

"Yeah," I gesture over to the sofa in front of us and take a step forward, sucking in a breath at the ache burning up my leg.

"Do you need a hand?" he asks, concern flickering in his eyes when he peers down at my leg.

I shake my head. "Just pulled a muscle at the gym," I force out as I reach the sofa and sink down into the worn cushions. Relief floods the pained nerves in my leg.

"Izzy says you're a personal trainer now," He settles beside me. The way he says her name so easily irritates the hell out of me.

"Almost." I grit my teeth. The fact that Izzy has already talked to him makes me uneasy. "What else did she tell you?"

"She told me you had no idea about her finding me. That you've been working hard and you're really passionate about the fitness stuff. She thinks it suits you, and by the looks of you, kid, I agree," he says, smacking a heavy palm onto my shoulder. I stare at his hand on my shoulder until it drops, then look away. "I'm proud of you. That probably means jack shit coming from some guy who's practically a stranger, but I am."

I blink, my mind momentarily taken back by his words. They hit deeper than I expect. He's right; they shouldn't mean anything coming from the man that abandoned me, but fuck, I hate how bad I needed to hear them.

I clear my throat and shift my weight on the couch. "It's more than Nora's ever told me."

"It was that bad, huh?"

I let out a short breath, jaw tightening. "I didn't die—" I shrug, like that's supposed to mean something "—so I guess it could've been worse."

His expression changes, like something cracks just under the surface. The tension in his jaw loosens, his eyes glossing over as he looks at me—really *looks* at me. His mouth opens, like he's about to say something, but nothing comes out. Then his shoulders start to shake. He drags his hands over his face, covering his mouth, trying to hold it in—but a broken breath slips through as he sobs.

I just sit there for a second, thrown off. Not sure what the hell to do with this. My hand lifts before I can stop it, landing awkwardly on his shoulder. I give it a brief squeeze, then drop it just as quick.

"I should have taken you with me." His voice cracks, the words barely making it out. "I knew it... but what life could I have given you on the road?"

He chokes on a breath, wiping at his face like he's trying to pull himself together. "At least here you had a roof over your head." His shoulders shake. "But I should have done so much more." His voice breaks, like the words barely make it out. He drags his hand down his face, shaking his head. "I'm sorry, K.C."

His apology hangs in the air between us.

I've spent years imagining what I'd say if I ever saw him again. None of those versions involved him sitting here barely holding it together and his voice breaking over my name.

And the worst part?

I want to believe him.

I slide my hand off him, the contact suddenly feeling like too much. "I'm okay," I say with a shrug. "Who knows? I probably wouldn't be me without all of this, right?" I glance away. "At least Nora is finally getting help. I think."

"She could be so volatile back then. I can only imagine." He drags a hand over his face again. "She wasn't always like that. When we first met...before the drinking, she was—"

"Sane?" I wonder aloud, doubtful that Nora was never not Nora.

"I know nothing I say or do all these years later can erase the way I left you... and the burden I put on your shoulders. But if you let me... I want to make this right."

I drag both hands over my head. "I don't even know what right looks like." And it hits me like a weight on my chest, how bad the kid inside of me needed to hear this from him... but the scars run too deep.

Izzy flashes through my mind. The future I still want with her, one that isn't defined by any of this, but by my choice to let go of it all and move forward.

His face falls and I say, "But we can try."

He nods slowly. "I'd really like that." He drags a hand over the back of his neck, silence stretching between us until the corner of his lip tugs up, like something just came to him. "You might have been too young to remember our little Sunday morning tradition."

"If it ain't Annamarie's—" I start, the words easily replaying in my mind what the sign above the door said.

"—it ain't breakfast," he finishes.

We used to wake up early and drive thirty minutes north just to beat the crowds and order their stuffed french toast.

"We could start with breakfast and go from there. What do you say?" he asks, hopeful.

Just as I'm about to respond, a loud knock interrupts us. Both of us turn our heads to the sound as the door knob turns.

"Hey, it's me!" Damon calls out from behind the door, slowly pushing it open. "If ya'll are naked and getting nasty, tell me now!" he yells, looking down as he steps inside, letting the door swing shut behind him. He stops short when he looks up, noticing us in the living room. "Well, this was not what I was expecting." He stares, dumbstruck at the person to my side. "You never texted me. I was just checking in. You good?" he asks, his gaze flicking between the two of us.

I pull myself up, dragging my bad leg under me. "Yeah, I'm alright. Thanks for checking in. This is my—" The word *dad* catches in my throat.

"Keagan. Senior. Obviously the older, better-looking version of Junior here." He chuckles as he stands, offering Damon his hand.

Damon steps up to shake his hand. The look on his face is stern/intense as he eyes him up and down. "I wish I could say it's nice to meet you, but I've known Chase too long for that."

"And I don't blame you," Keagan replies. "Glad he's got good people around him." He turns toward me with a small smile. "Well, I'll get out of the way here."

Reaching into his back pocket as he walks around Damon, he pulls out a business card and sets it on the coffee table. "Breakfast whenever you're ready, son."

I nod, watching as he slowly backs toward the door. He lingers for a moment with his hand on the knob before finally turning it and stepping out.

The door clicks shut and all I can do is stare after him. *Did that really just happen?*

Damon clasps my shoulder in his hand, squeezing reassuringly. "You okay?" he asks, concern etched on his face.

"Yeah," I say as my gaze is still stuck on the door. "Izzy found him."

Damon collapses onto the couch beside me, his voice surprised. "I didn't even know you were trying to find him."

"I wasn't." I admit, sinking back into the cushions.

I scrub a hand over my face.

"Uh-oh...what did you do?"

I look over at Damon. His eyes are narrowed, studying me.

"I flipped out on her and now..." I sigh, rubbing my face, her voicemail from earlier replaying in my mind. My stomach sinks at the thought of being reduced to a friend, of losing her and what we have. She's opened my eyes and my heart to things I never knew I could have and feel. And I fucked it all up.

"I mean your anger was warranted," Damon says carefully. "But maybe not with the girl you love."

"I know," I mutter.

"Okay," he says, leaning forward like he's ready for a plan. "So what are you going to do about it?"

Determination hits me, cutting through the dense fog I've been in.

"I need to apologize. I need to make this right. I need to get my girl."

"But first—" Damon points to my leg. "You need to ice that thing, dummy, before it falls off."

I follow his gaze at the back of my leg. The muscle is already swelling and a bruise is starting to spread under my skin.

Shit. "That doesn't look good."

Damon snorts. "You think?"

12

IZZY

It's officially been twenty-four hours. Somewhere between late afternoon and evening, I lost track of time, checking my phone for the umpteenth time, hoping for a message or a missed call. As expected, my texts are still on read and there is no sign of him reaching out. I promised to give him space but my heart sinks at the realization that this is the longest we've gone without speaking.

This silence leaves a hollow ache in my chest.

As the hours drag on, my anxiety only gets worse. I keep replaying the look on his face when he asked me to leave, and the way he could barely walk when I left.

Feeling restless and more than a little nervous, I finally grab my keys and head to the gym. Maybe he'll be there. Maybe we can get this confrontation over with once and for all.

We're either working through this... or we're not, right?

My stomach twists at the possibility that we might not be.

This is what I get for being a chismosa, as Ma would say, and sticking my nose where it had no business being.

Mya told me last night to give him space. To let him cool off.

But twenty-four hours of silence later, patience feels a lot like torture and I can't take another second in the dark.

I deliberately drive past his house, hopeful that his empty parking spot out front means he is in fact working out his frustrations at the gym like I thought. The knot in my stomach tightens as I turn at the end of the block and head toward the main road.

My grip tightens on the steering wheel as the sun dips low, painting the sky in shades of orange and pink. I pull into the gym parking lot, the fading light casting long shadows across the pavement. My eyes scan the rows of cars in the plaza, searching for his color Jeep.

But it's nowhere to be seen.

I draw in a slow breath, trying to calm the nerves twisting in my stomach.

This is dumb.

With sweaty palms, I push the heavy gym door open and manage a quick smile at Bri behind the desk while scanning my member ID.

"Hey," she says brightly. "Just you today?"

Her question bursts the small bubble of hope I had been holding onto.

"I guess so," I respond, not even trying to hide the disappointment in my voice.

My eyes roam the open gym anyway. The scent of sweat and rubber fills my nostrils as I take in the rows of exercise equipment and sounds of weights clanking together. All as it should be minus one very tall, blonde, and broad-chested trainer.

"Have a good work out!" Bri calls out as I walk away.

I wish I could just blend in with the crowd and escape into my own world of physical exertion but all I see is Chase here— in every corner, in every reflection, in every part of this place that was where it all started. Sadness wraps itself around my heart, pulling tight with each step I take.

As I pass the row of treadmills and glance at our usual training area, I spot Damon walking into the locker room. Forcing my feet forward, I decide against stopping to ask him about Chase and make a bee line for the stairs to the second-floor track instead.

The indoor track stretches out in front of me, only two other runners circling the loop. I barely register their presence as I pop my earbuds into my ears and pull my leg behind me in a quick stretch. The gentle pull in the front of my right thigh feels good, relieving some tension before switching to the other.

The smooth melody of The Marias fills my ears, my feet falling into sync to the beat of the song, pulling me further into my head. Before long, I'm jogging, lost in a rhythm that feels almost like meditation. The steady thud of my feet against the rubberized surface drowns out the chaos in my heart, but my mind still replays the events that have landed us here.

Every lap brings another memory. Another flash of Chase. His laugh. The way he looks at me when he thinks I'm not paying attention.

I shake my head, pushing myself harder, my lungs burning as if they might burst. My labored breath feels heavy with disappointment and frustration as I try to focus on the track in front of me, but all I think about is him. I slow down, the burn in my legs catching up to me when I come to a stop. I bend over, hands braced on my knees as I drag in deep breaths. Looking around, I realize I'm the only one up here. I swipe at the sweat dripping down my forehead when the row of lights above me suddenly start to turn off.

"Hey! I'm still up here!" I call out, running over to the railing that runs along the center of the track. I pull my earbuds out of my ear and peer down into the darkened lower level, panic slowly washing over me.

"Damon!" I call out. "Bri?"

Nothing but the faint outline of abandoned equipment. The glow of street lights in the parking lot spill through the large floor-to-ceiling windows, the only light filtering in.

My stomach drops.

No! No, no, no.

This cannot be happening to me!

I sprint down the stairs, my footsteps echoing harshly against concrete as panic crawls up my spine. Ignoring the burning in my calves, I run until I reach the front doors, and yank at the handle.

Locked.

I press my head against the cool tempered glass, wracking my brain for who to call. I don't have Damon's phone number. I'm left with no other choice but to call Chase.

"Please pick up, please pick up, please pick up," I beg, my heart racing as I wait for the phone to ring. And then I hear the unmistakable chime of a phone behind me.

Holding my breath as my deepest fears become a sudden reality, I slowly turn toward the sound. A looming figure leans against the reception desk—tall, broad shoulders, intimidating in a way that makes my pulse stutter.

I scream.

Then I look closer.

"Chase," I gasp, clutching my chest. Relief washes over me, but it's quickly replaced by a rush of anger *because what in the actual fuck.*

"You literally scared me half to death!" I snap, taking a few steps toward him.

He doesn't say anything. In the dim light spilling through the windows, his face is mostly shadowed, but I can still feel his eyes on me. Even with a good eight-feet between us, they drag over me like a touch, taking in my flushed skin, the sweat still clinging to my neck, the rise and fall of my chest as I try to catch my breath.

He pushes off of the desk and takes slow steps toward me. I can't help noticing the slight drag of his left leg, still sore from yesterday, I imagine. My breath catches as he closes the distance between us, head tilting back to meet his gaze. The intensity in his eyes sends a shiver down my spine.

And this is it.

My mind flashes back to when we first met—when I jokingly accused him of being a serial killer.

This is the moment he kills me, isn't it?

Or worse... breaks my heart.

I'll survive this. I've done it before, I remind myself.

He leans down, his forehead touching mine. The warmth from his body envelops me, burning me up from the inside out. I search his eyes, trying to read the emotions swirling within them.

"Chase," I whisper between us. I can't tell if he wants to kiss me or murder me right now.

"Friends, Izzy?" His voice is rough as the corners of his eyes pinch together. "Do you really think I could ever be friends with you?"

"Then what do you want, Chase?" My voice trembles slightly.

He shakes his head, studying me for a moment longer, the intensity in his eyes deepening as one hand slides up my thigh and under my shirt. "You know what I want," he says, his breath brushing against my lips.

My eyes flutter shut. "But I don't. You ghosted me instead of talking."

"I love you. I know saying it is not enough, and I'm sorry for how I handled yesterday." He shakes his head, jaw tightening. "I've got issues, baby. Terrible fucking coping skills, and more baggage than I can deal with—" his eyes hold mine "—but I love you. I could never go back to life before you. You're the light when I'm stuck in the dark, Izzy. You're the reason I want to fight through my past and I've never wanted to fight for anything as much as I want to fight for you. For us."

His words pulse under my skin, igniting a fire that spreads through me, weaving through the doubts and fears I've carried these last twenty four hours.

"Oh," I manage, my voice barely above a whisper.

"Oh?" He echoes.

"That's not what I was expecting."

"What were you expecting?"

"For you to break my heart and kick me to the curb."

He shakes his head, smiling slightly, but pulling me into his arms.

"I don't ever want to break your heart, Izzy. If anyone deserves to be kicked to the curb here, it's me."

"No, I don't want that either," I say, wrapping my arms around his neck.

"I'm sorry."

"Me too." I lean back so I can look him in the eyes and apologize. "Really, Chase. I was out of line and I am so sorry."

"Shh." His thumb brushes over my lips "I've listened to your voicemail at least a hundred times by now. I know, babe."

A small smile pulls at his mouth. "Can we skip to the kiss and make up part now?" he mutters. "Because I don't want to go another second without my lips on yours."

I nod my head eagerly, waiting for his mouth to meet mine. His tongue parts my lips and my body doesn't waste a second melting into him. All the tension of the day fades away, replaced by his touch. His hands roam my back, pulling me closer and I lose myself to him while the word around us fades into nothingness.

"We probably shouldn't be doing this here," I let out, breathless.

"You're right." He untangles himself from me, takes my hand, and pulls me along as he guides us through the dark gym. We weave past rows of machines until he pushes open the door to the men's locker room.

The fluorescent lights flicker on overhead.

A row of sinks stretches along one wall, a long mirror running the length above them. Behind us, the tiled showers sit empty and silent.

Chase releases me quickly to turn one of the showers on. Water bursts from the showerhead and steam begins to curl into the air.

A second later, he pulls me back against him, guiding us in front of the large mirror. Our bodies press together in the reflection, his broad frame nearly swallowing mine.

"I've had this fantasy of you here," he murmurs, his voice low against my ear. He dips his head, burying his face in the crook of my neck. "You let out this little moan during our first workout together," he admits quietly. "I couldn't get that sound out of my head."

The memory of that night rushes back, when we were nothing more than innocent touches here or there.

His eyes sweep over me as one hand squeezes my hip before sliding under the hem of my t-shirt.

"Why do you look at me like that?" I ask, catching his gaze in the mirror behind us. His eyes drag over me —slow, deliberate — like he's seeing something I don't. "I look like a bum in shorts and an oversized t-shirt."

He chuckles, shaking his head. "You could wear a potato sack, and I'd still look at you like this." His unwavering gaze never leaves mine as his hand inches higher up my side.

The gentle brush of his knuckles against my skin makes me suck in a breath.

I stop his hand from lifting my shirt. "Promise me there is zero chance of anyone walking in here."

"Alarm is set, doors are locked, there are no cameras in the locker room and Damon left me his keys. It's just you and me, Izzy." His lips brush my shoulder, then the side of my neck, peppering slow kisses along my skin.

He pauses just long enough to meet my eyes in the mirror, silently asking.

Trusting him, I let my fears go and drop my hand. He pulls fabric upward, lifting my shirt over my head and tossing it aside. His other hand glides down the side of my body, over my soft belly before slipping into the waistband of my bike shorts.

A shiver runs through me as his hard length presses against my lower back. Behind us, the shower continues to run, steam creeping across the mirror in front of us.

"Chase..." I whisper, though it comes out more like a breath than a word.

My palms brace against the sink, his body flush against mine.

"I need these off," he mutters. His hand slips from my shorts, hooking his fingers into the waistband and pulling them down over my hips. I kick off my sneakers and step out of them as the fabric slides the rest of the way down my legs.

His breath warms the back of my skin, sending a ripple of goosebumps down my spine.

"Fuck, Izzy," he groans, the words thick with desire.

The sound shoots straight to my core. It's been a bit longer than twenty-four hours since we last touched but my body feels starved for him.

His large hands envelop my body with a burning touch, molding me like clay. His fingertips bring me to life as one hand slips between my folds while the other battles with the zipper of my sports bra.

"Take this off," he says, nipping at my skin with his teeth. My mind, too disoriented, struggles to send the signals to my arms, which cling to him for support.

"Izzy," he urges.

Right. Bra. Off.

With effort, I force my heavy limbs into action and unzip my sports bra. Behind me, Chase wastes no time kicking off his sneakers and stripping out of the rest of his clothes. I let the bra drop to the floor in front of me as my breasts fall free. Chase wraps an arm around me, greedily trying to catch both in his arms while his other hand continues where it left off on my clit.

"Look at you," he whispers. "God, you're incredible, Izzy."

"Hmm," I moan, imagining the sight rather than opening my eyes.

"Open your eyes, baby. I want you to see what I see."

As I open them, the reflection in the mirror takes my breath away. The sight of me bare in his arms, his fingers possessively on my breasts, framing my body as if I were a masterpiece and he the sculptor. I've never felt so completely claimed, as if every part of me belonged to him and him alone.

The way he gazes at my reflection, hunger and admiration mixed in his eyes, sends a thrill through me. The curve of my hips, the way my body melts back into his touch, trusting his hands to hold me there. It's almost too much, but I can't look away. Because what's in that mirror isn't just me—it's us.

"I love how you look in my arms," he whispers. "But I love how you taste on my tongue so much more," he says. He tightens his hold on me and guides us both under the spray of the hot water. The shower head sits high above him, the stream hitting the back of his head before cascading over his shoulders and down the hard planes of his chest.

I bite down on my lower lip, watching the droplets trace their way over his skin. Without thinking, I step closer, my lips finding the center of his chest. The taste of salt and warm water hits my tongue as I press a slow kiss there, my teeth grazing lightly along his skin.

He sucks in a sharp breath when my teeth catch on his pebbled nipple. His hand tightens on my hip while the other reaches for my ponytail, tugging just enough to tilt my head back and force my gaze up to his. He lowers himself to me, capturing my mouth in a deep, devouring kiss.

My body melts into his, chest pressed to his upper abs as the water runs over us both. My back meets the cool tile of the shower wall as he crowds into my space. I wrap one leg around his waist, desperate to climb him, to pull him closer and feel every inch of him inside me. He takes my wrists in one hand, guiding them above my head, holding them there. The position forces my chest forward and the look he gives me nearly undoes me when he pulls back, his eyes dark with intensity that make my pulse race. Heat floods my face as this wild, aching need for him, for all of him, consumes me.

I rock my hips forward desperate for his cock. He pushes against me, pressing into my belly. Instead of giving me what I want, he takes his time. His mouth drags slowly along the curve of my breast before he closes around my nipple, sucking hard. He releases it with a pop and moves on to the other one.

My head falls back against the tile. The tension inside of me coils tight. I don't know how much more I can take.

"Chase," I gasp, pushing against his hold. "Please."

His answering smile is slow and wicked as if he really is trying to torture me. He releases my arms and then lowers himself, hands sliding along my hips as he sinks down in front of me. In the next second, he has my legs wrapped around his head, lifting me against the wall. My breath catches in my throat as his tongue swirls around my swollen nub. My fingers grip the edge of the low tile behind me as his shoulders support me as if I was weightless, the steam curling around.

I'm so intoxicated by his touch, his searing tongue, *him*. I'm lost in the rhythm of his mouth. Each lick sends jolts of ecstasy through me, building inside of me until I'm on the brink of shattering in his hands.

He moans against me, the sound humming through me as a finger enters my center, curling inside of me and reaching the exact spot that sends me over. I grip the back of his head, clawing his shoulders and neck as wave after wave of pleasure washes over me. My cries bounce off the walls, echoing around us as he relentlessly devours me. I feel limp in his arms as he untangles my legs from his shoulders one at a time, lowering me right onto his waiting cock.

"I love you," he breathes, kissing my lips. We moan into each other's mouths as he slides into me, filling me completely. My legs tighten around him, holding on as his hips rock in and out, over and over in a slow torrent. It isn't long before the sweet pressure inside of me begins to build up again.

He leans back, bringing me with him, his hands gripping my thighs as he pushes me down over him, covering my cries with his lips. The feeling is too intense, too deep. Our bodies are slick with water. His chest clings to my breasts as we move together, lost in each other.

Our breaths are ragged as the tension builds, and we both find our release crashing over us. "I love you," I cry into his mouth, shaking and collapsing over him, my arms hanging over his shoulders and head falling into his neck.

His heartbeat gradually slows beneath my cheek, as does mine, and I savor this feeling in his arms. My eyes drift to our reflection in the mirror across the showers. Despite the light fog, we're a beautiful mess of intertwining limbs, a blend of soft and hard bodies, seamlessly fused together with no beginning or end.

"Yeah, we could never be friends," I whisper, biting my lip as a smile tugs at the corners of my mouth.

"Hopefully this brought you to your senses." He lifts my chin gently, his gaze locking onto mine "And you don't ever question us again." He presses a soft kiss to my lips. "This is real, remember?"

"How could I ever forget?"

CHASE

After finally taking a real shower and locking up the gym, we make it back to her apartment where sleep is the last thing on our minds.

We end up tangled up in her bed, sheets twisted around our legs, Izzy tucked into the crook of my arm, exactly where she belongs. The room is quiet except for the soft hum of the ceiling fan and the steady rhythm of her breathing against my chest.

My calf protests every time I shift, the muscle still tight as hell, but there are worse ways to recover than with Izzy draped all over me. Because this right here, having Izzy back in my arms, makes everything in my world feel right again. Her light and warmth add to the void inside of me, filling the empty spaces I didn't know could be filled. She's the refuge to my heart, the home I've always wished for.

"You won't believe who showed up at my door."

"Not Nora," she asks, pushing herself up onto her elbow.

I shake my head. "Mr. Keagan O'Rourke, the first in the flesh."

Her hand flies to her mouth, eyes widening. "I-I didn't think he would just show up. I didn't give him your number or—"

I stop her with a quick kiss. "It's okay," I say, shaking my head.

"No, it's not." She shakes her head, guilt written all over her face. "I had no business contacting him and forcing him to show up like that. I'm so sorry, Chase."

I brush a strand of hair off her shoulder. "Hey. I am your business."

She studies my face like she's trying to figure out if I really mean that.

"It wasn't bad," I continue. "I mean... I was shocked. Thought it was you at first. Oh, and I might've swung on him after letting him in." I shrug. "But it wasn't terrible. Kinda like ripping a Band-Aid off."

"Did you talk?" she asks softly.

I let out a slow breath, staring up at the ceiling for a second. "Yeah."

Her fingers trace slow circles on my chest while she waits.

"He apologized," I tell her. "Like... really apologized. Broke down and everything."

Her hand pauses.

"And?"

"And I didn't know what the hell to do with that," I admit.

A small smile touches her lips. "It's a start," she says.

I huff out a quiet laugh.

"And what about breakfast?" she asks.

I narrow my eyes at her. "How much did you two talk before you finally told me?"

"Just once. He mentioned something about Sundays and stuffed French toast."

"Yeah." I say quietly. The thought of her talking to him still rubs me the wrong way.

She's quiet for a moment. "Do you want to go?"

The answer sits heavy in my chest for a second.

Then I look down at her and nod. "Yeah," I say. "I think I do."

"Tell me something I don't know about you," she announces.

"Okay." I think for a second. "I've never had alcohol before."

"Eh, not surprised... but you were never curious?"

I shake my head. "Nope, I had this fucked up idea that one sip would turn me into Nora."

"That makes sense, but we're not our parents, babe, or their mistakes." She pauses, her palm covering my jaw. "You're not Nora, or your father. You're you, and you get to decide who you want to be."

Her words slowly sink in before she fills the space with a confession of her own.

"I'm scared I'm going to lose myself to another relationship."

Her words send a quick jolt of alarm through me and my heart leaps. I rub my hand up and down her spine, needing to touch and remind her that *hey, it's me here*—no one else, definitely not her ex. "I won't let you." I kiss her nose before continuing, "I don't want this to feel like a sacrifice for you."

Her lips press into my chin as she places her hand on my chest. "I think I'm learning that with you."

"Good. We both have a lot to learn and unlearn." I tuck her under my chin.

"Maybe our love can be us growing together instead of losing ourselves in each other."

"Mhm, but I do like losing myself in you." A smile spreads across my face, Izzy giggling as my hand slips under the covers. When I find her side and tickle her, she bursts into laughter, screaming and trying to squirm away from me.

I press myself between her legs, shushing her with my mouth. "Shh, you're going to wake your neighbors."

She wraps her arms around my neck. "You weren't worried about my neighbors earlier."

I lean down, hovering above her lips. "Baby, I'm not worried about anybody else when I'm inside you. The world can be burning and I wouldn't care. Between your thighs isn't a bad way to die or get the cops called on us."

"You're crazy," she laughs.

"For you," I finish, capturing her lips. Her mouth melts against mine as I deepen the kiss, quickly losing myself in her.

"Babe—" she groans, pulling away slightly "We really need sleep."

I glance at the clock behind her. The faint glow of 3:00 AM illuminates the dark. A huff escapes me as my mind starts calculating down to the minutes until I have to leave this bed. Dropping my forehead against Izzy's, I know she's right. I fall back into the pillow beside her and pull her closer to me, wishing like hell I could just freeze time and stay here with her forever.

"So, we sleep," I say, closing my eyes.

"I love you."

"I love you, Isadora." I brush my thumb along her arm. A beat of silence. "Will you come with me to visit Nora next week?"

"Of course, I will."

I pull her closer against my chest. "Thank you. Now sleep, woman."

It feels like I have just closed my eyes when the sound of my alarm tears me from sleep a few hours later. With Izzy still tucked in my arm undisturbed by the blaring sound, I lean over her, stretching my other arm out and grabbing my phone from the nightstand, silencing it with a quick tap.

"Five more minutes," she mumbles sleepily, her arms and legs wrapping around me, and pulling me down over her. I let her cling to me, burying my face in the crook of her neck, inhaling the sweet scent of her hair and savoring the warmth of her skin.

If I didn't have to drive back to my place to get ready for work at the veterinary hospital, I'd happily stay, but... "I have to run home before work. I'll reset your alarm for you, okay?" I whisper, gently brushing a strand of hair from her face before untangling myself from her. I get up from the bed and start the hunt for my clothes on the floor.

She shakes her head. "No, I need to be at school early to set up for our end of year party," she says, with her eyes still closed and showing no intention of getting out of bed.

I can't help feeling a twinge of guilt for keeping her up so late, but we were both so wired after everything.

"Izzy," I say softly, tugging my t-shirt over my head. I struggle against the urge to let her sleep, knowing she needs to start her day, too.

"I'm up," she says, sitting up and stretching her arms over her head. The bedsheet slips down, revealing her plump breasts.

Momentarily distracted, I can't help but stare while I fumble with one shoe.

"Good morning," she says, catching my gaze.

"It is a good morning," I respond, watching her as she throws the sheets aside and walks toward me. Her hips sway and every enticing curve on her body is on full display.

I love seeing her like this, that glimmer in her dark eyes, her body like a fire drawing me. As she reaches me, she stands on her tiptoes, wrapping her arms around my neck while my eager hands glide along her soft belly. She stands on her tiptoes to kiss me. My brain thinks long and hard about all the ways to get out of going into work today.

"You should just move in," she says, her words freezing me in place.

Tilting my head to the side, and replaying her words in my head, I ask, "What?" convinced I heard her wrong.

"Move in, here with me," she repeats, her eyes steady on mine, a small smile on her lips.

My heart pounds in my chest as I search her eyes for any inkling of doubt. There is none. "That would be crazy," I say, running the pad of my thumb over her bottom lip.

"Oh, my bad, I just thought we were crazy in love or something." She looks away, lowering back onto her heels as she starts to pull away, but I catch her, pulling her back into my arms and lifting her off her feet.

"Madly," I whisper, pressing a soft kiss to her lips. "But what about not losing yourself to us? You're just getting your footing after fuck-face."

She smiles knowingly. "My feet—" she pauses, gently pushing away from me, resting her palms on my chest as she stands back down on the ground "—have never been more planted on the ground."

"Is that so?" I smile down at her.

"It is. Besides, I've decided I'm throwing caution to the wind, babe. I want you here."

I search her face out of habit, waiting for the doubt to creep in–for her to come back to her senses–it doesn't.

"And I want to be here."

"Good. Now you can finally put that key I gave you to use," she says with a teasing smile playing across her lips.

I raise an eyebrow, pulling her tighter. "I gave you a key, too."

"But you're always here," she counters. "You might as well just stay."

"Okay." I let her go, grabbing my sweater and shrugging it on.

"Okay?" she asks, tying her robe right around her waist.

"Yeah," I say, sitting back down on the bed to put my other sneaker on. A sense of calm washes over me. This is a huge decision. I've never lived with any other woman but Nora, and the thought of taking this step, with Izzy, feels like coming home.

"I'll bring some stuff over tonight and figure out the house stuff later. Talk to my Dad about putting the house up for sale."

"Really?" She stops in front of me.

"Come here." She steps between my thighs, my hands instinctively finding their way back to her waist. I pull her close, until I'm resting my chin in the center of her chest. "Under one condition. When your lease is up, we find a place we can make our own together. One that will have both of our names on the lease. Deal?"

"Deal."

"Are you sure?" I ask, searching her eyes again. I need her to be sure.

"I've never been more sure about anything or anyone, Chase. I got you and you got me, right?" And it's true. I can finally see it in her face, hear it in her voice.

A slow grin pulls at my lips, a steady kind of happiness settling deep in my chest.

"Always."

14

IZZY

Sitting in the medical rehabilitation wing of the county detention center's waiting room, tension radiates off me like a heatwave. My heart pounds and my leg bounces against the linoleum floor, fingers twisting together in my lap. The thick scent of Febreze hangs in the air, trying—and failing—to mask the underlying smell of antiseptic and something sour I can't quite place.

I can't help stealing glances around at the other visitors, their despondent stares stuck on the floor or the walls. They took all personal items at check-in, so with no phones to distract us, the walls are slowly closing in on me. I brace myself for what's to come. For who's to come.

Nora.

It's not that I'm nervous. Quite the opposite, in fact, as the thought of finally meeting this woman puts me on edge in a way I don't like. Her name alone literally makes my stomach churn. A rush of anger bubbles just beneath the surface, igniting this fierce protectiveness for Chase.

God, what would I say to her if I let my emotions take the reins here? The things I'd really like to tell her are definitely not acceptable words for my boyfriend's mother, but they are what someone should have t ld this woman a long ass time ago.

"Hey." Chase's hand closes around mine, gently dragging my knuckles up to his lips and placing a soft kiss. Warmth immediately spreads through me. He can instantly calm any storm raging inside me.

"Why do you look like someone just kicked your dog?" he asks, a teasing smile tugging at the corners of his mouth while he rests his chin on the top of my knuckles.

I let out a small laugh, taking in his warm gaze and relaxed demeanor; a stark contrast to the last time we were in a waiting room together. Back then, shadows clung to his eyes. It's almost hard to believe the man in front of me is the same one who had been so weighed down by his past, by her. This version radiates inner strength, peace, and confidence.

I hope Nora chokes on it.

"I'm nervous," I confess.

"Of Nora? Don't be. This is just a means to an end, babe."

"Yeah, I know..." I say, swallowing down the image of me swinging on her. "How do you think she's going to react to you selling the house?"

"Doesn't matter. She hasn't paid a damn bill there since I was ten."

"O'Rourke?"

"That's us," Chase says, dragging me up with him. We walk toward the man holding the doors open and he smiles as we meet him.

"I'm Joe Ilaqcua, your mother's caseworker," he says, stretching his hand out. Chase shakes his hand.

"Nice to meet you. This is Izzy, my girlfriend." I shake his hand as he cocks his head to the side, eyeing us.

"She never mentioned a girlfriend."

"Well, she's never really taken an interest in me unless I was taking care of her after a bender, so…"

The caseworker nods his head before turning down the hallway. "Point taken. Please, follow me."

We walk past a series of closed doors, fluorescent lights humming overhead.

"Look…" Joe begins carefully. "I know you and your mother have had some… difficulties."

"*Difficulties?*" The word slips out before I can stop it. "You clearly don't know anything about him or what she put him through."

Chase's arm slides around my waist, gently pulling me into his side.

"Sorry," I mutter.

He presses a kiss to the top of my head. "Don't be."

Joe sighs softly. "My mother was an addict my entire life," he says. "So, I do understand more than most. But what I'm about to say isn't easy to hear."

We stop outside a door at the end of the hall.

"Your mother isn't well," Joe continues. "And frankly… there's no way to sugarcoat this." He looks directly at Chase. "She's dying."

I turn my head to gauge Chase's reaction.

His face barely changes.

"Yeah," he says quietly. "Liver disease will do that when you treat vodka like water for twenty-six years."

Joe nods. "I understand the anger," he says carefully. "I see it a lot in situations like this." He pauses, like he's choosing his words. "All I can say is... if there's something you need to say to her, it might be worth saying it now." His gaze softens. "What you carry after this—it stays with you."

Chase's jaw tightens. "Can we see her now?"

"Of course." Joe pushes the door open, stepping aside to let us in. "I'll be right out here," he says quietly, giving us a moment before easing the door mostly closed behind us.

The first thing I notice is that the hospital room smells faintly of antiseptic and stale air. The second is Nora O'Rourke, lying against the white sheets like a ghost of herself.

Her skin is tinged a sickly yellow, stretched thin over a body that looks half the size it probably once was.

Fragile.

Hollow.

This is Nora.

The woman who's made Chase's life hell.

And standing here now...all I feel is pity.

"Keagan," she croaks.

"No, Nora, it's me, Chase."

"Of course it's you, pumpkin." She coughs. "You cut your hair... You know you look better with more hair on your head."

"Good to see you, too." Chase's jaw ticks, his face going carefully blank like he's forcing himself not to react.

"I'm kidding. When'd you get so serious?"

"Nora, this is Izzy—my girlfriend."

I bite my tongue and force a polite smile as I extend my hand toward her.

Instead of taking it, she just stares at me. Her eyes flick between my face and Chase's before her hand suddenly flies to her mouth. A violent fit of coughing overtakes her, her thin shoulders shaking with the effort.

I slowly lower my hand, rubbing it against my thigh instead.

Nora keeps her eyes on Chase, like I'm not even standing there.

"You look good, pumpkin," she rasps, her voice thin from the coughing. "Different... but good."

She doesn't glance my way once.

Chase shifts beside me and I feel the subtle tightening of his hand around mine.

"That's Izzy," Chase says, nodding toward me. "We're in love."

His gaze finds mine, and my cheeks warm as my insides melt under the intensity of his gaze. I glance at Nora just in time to see her expression shift, her eyes glistening.

"Love?" she scoffs. "You don't actually believe that shit."

"Yeah, Nora. I do." Chase's voice stays steady, unwavering.

Nora looks away, shaking her head. "Love doesn't last, Chase. Before you know it, you'll be walking out that door just like your father."

Chase's jaw tightens. "You know what? Maybe that's true for you," he says calmly. "But it doesn't have to be my story. I'm not him, and I'm not going anywhere. Love is a choice, Nora. It's something you build, not something you abandon."

Nora's eyes flash with anger, but something hides deep beneath it.

"Build?" she snaps. "You think it's that easy? You don't know the cost of sticking around when everything falls apart."

"I know more than you think," Chase replies. "I watched you crumble. I watched my childhood disappear because of it." His voice stays level, but the words cut deeply. "But I'm choosing something different.

"What?" Nora lets out a bitter laugh. "You think love's gonna fix you? Please. Don't be so naïve."

I step forward before I can stop myself.

"Love isn't going to fix anything," I say, my voice calm but firm. "We're far from perfect. But we're committed to each other, even when things get hard." I glance at Chase, a small smile breaking through the tension. "It's about showing up. Even when it's messy."

"That's cute," Nora mutters.

Chase doesn't take the bait. "I'm selling the house," he says, cutting through the tense room like a blade.

Nora's head snaps up. "You can't do that."

"I can."

Her face crumples just enough to look fragile, her voice dropping into something softer.

"I'm sick, pumpkin," she gasps. "I'm dying. That house is my home, you can't just—"

"Home?" Chase cuts in. "That place has been my prison since the day you brought me home from the hospital."

The room goes still.

"I'm selling the house," he says, slowly.

"You can't."

"I can. The house is still in Dad's name, and he already said he'd sign it over to me."

"Your dad?" she spits. "You saw that piece of shi—"

Her words dissolve into another violent fit of coughing.

The door opens up behind her and Joe rushes to her side.

"Okay, okay," he says gently. "Let's take a breath for a moment." He turns to Nora. "Nora, remember what you shared with me earlier."

Nora sags back against the pillows with a tired sigh. "I know I've been a shit mom," she says hoarsely. "And I'm sorry. I wish... in another life... I could've done better." Her eyes lift to Chase. "I'm dying, and I can't bear the thought of you hating me for the rest of your life."

Chase doesn't move. "I don't hate you, Nora," he says quietly. "I don't feel anything."

The words land heavy in the room.

"You barely raised me," he continues. "You just taught me how to take care of myself, so I could take care of you."

Nora nods slowly, like she expected that answer.

"Good," she murmurs. "Sell the house then. What's it matter to me? I'll probably be dead before the end of the week anyway."

"Yeah," Chase says, unfazed. "You could be."

For the first time since we walked into this place, he looks lighter—like something he's carried for years finally slipped off his shoulders.

Nora studies him for a long moment, her eyes glassy. "I'm sorry," she whispers again. "I never wanted to hurt you."

Chase shakes his head. "I don't know what you wanted," he says. "But I'm done carrying it."

Silence settles over the room. Joe clears his throat gently. "I think that's enough for today."

Chase nods once, then reaches for my hand. We turn toward the door.

"Chase," Nora calls weakly.

He pauses but doesn't turn around.

"Just... promise me one thing."

He glances back over his shoulder. "What?"

Her gaze drifts to me. "Take care of her," she says softly. "Love her better than I ever loved anyone."

Chase's hand tightens around mine. "I already do."

As we step into the hallway, I can barely process what just happened. We walk in silence past the heavy doors of the medical wing until we reach the small security desk near the entrance.

The officer behind the counter slides a plastic bin toward us. Our phones and keys sit inside, tagged with the same numbered card they gave us when we checked in.

Chase picks up his wallet and phone while I slip my phone back into my bag. The distant voices echo through the medical rehabilitation wing of the county detention center.

Neither of us say a word. We push through the final set of doors and step outside.

The moment we're outside, we turn toward each other like magnets. Chase's hand finds mine, grounding me as he pulls me back into his orbit.

"Are you okay?" I ask, searching his face for any sign of distress.

"I will be," he says, and there's a light in his eyes I've never seen before. "I finally feel free."

My chest tightens. "I'm proud of you," I whisper, squeezing his hand. "You did what you needed to do."

He pulls me closer, his arm settling around my waist. "I couldn't have done it without you."

We stand there for a moment in front of the entrance, the afternoon sun warm against our skin. "Ready?" I ask, tilting my head up at him.

"More than ever," he replies, a small smile breaking across his face.

His fingers tighten around mine as we start toward the parking lot together. And for the first time since I met him, the future doesn't feel heavy. It feels wide open.

This is what I want the rest of my life to look like, supporting each other through the moments that test us and coming out stronger than the day before.

EPILOGUE
CHASE

Ten months and three weeks later

"Keep going, Izzy!" I call out, my voice steady as I watch her struggle with the monster truck-sized tire.

"I can't! It's too big!" she grunts, her determination shining through the sweat glistening on her forehead.

"You can. Now, open your legs wider, baby." I keep my gaze locked on her, the heat of my stare fueling her resolve.

"Wider. There you go. That's it." Fire blazes in her eyes as she pushes with everything she has, and I can't help but feel proud. She's come so far this year, both physically and emotionally, and it's been incredible to witness.

With a final grunt, she sends the tire crashing down to the ground, and the look of triumph on her face is everything. "I told you you could do it," I say, wrapping my arms around her waist and lifting her effortlessly.

"Eww, stop, I'm all hot and sweaty," she protests, but I can't resist the urge to tease her.

"You know I like you wet, baby," I whisper in her ear, earning a playful glare.

"Hey, the gym floor is for working out, not making out. Y'all know this!" Damon calls out from across the room.

I reluctantly lower Izzy back down, stealing a quick kiss before turning my attention back to her. "Feel like a run?" I ask, already pulling her toward the treadmills.

"Hell no," she replies.

"You know you need to lower your heart rate. Just take a walk, then."

As I hop on the treadmill and kick it to life, I glance over at her, appreciating the way her muscles have toned and defined. She's a force of nature, and I'm lucky to be by her side.

"You okay back there?" I ask, my voice steady as I jog.

"Yup, just avoiding any unnecessary trauma to my head." She laughs, stepping onto the treadmill beside mine. In an instant, I lose my footing, my body hitting the floor with a thud.

"Chase!" Izzy gasps, hopping to my side. "Are you okay?"

Her voice trembles with panic as my eyes flutter open, my body still registering the impact. "Chase?" she calls again, and I can't help but smirk at the worry etched on her face.

"Damon!" she yells, but before he can come rushing over, I can't hold it in any longer. I break out into laughter, her expression shifting from concern to annoyance.

"What is wrong with you? I was so fucking worried!" she exclaims, smacking my chest, a mix of anger and relief washing over her.

"I'm sorry," I say, still chuckling as I wrap my hand around her wrist. My heart races as I push something into her palm, watching her confusion morph into disbelief.

"What are you—" she starts, but then her eyes widen when she stares down at the stunning ring I've placed in her hands—beautiful solitaire surrounded by smaller sparkling diamonds.

I kneel down in front of her, and her mouth falls open. "Holy shit," she breathes.

"I think you're supposed to be standing," I tease, taking the ring from her hands.

"Chase." Her voice is soft, tears brimming in her eyes.

I squeeze her right hand in mine, the warmth of her love radiating through me. "Isadora Leticia Peña Yotun De la Vega," I say, putting on my best accent. "Today marks exactly one year since you fell into my life. All it took was one look at you for me to know you were the home my heart's been searching for. The love I've spent my life begging for. I love you more—"

"Yes!" she interrupts, tears spilling down her cheeks. "Yes, yes, yes!" She spreads her fingers wide for me.

"I wasn't done," I say, grinning as I place the ring gently on her finger.

"I'm sorry," she says, cupping my jaw with her hands. "I just couldn't wait another second!"

As I pull her into my arms, the applause around us fades into the background. I press my forehead to hers, feeling the weight of the moment. "It doesn't matter," I whisper. "You already know what you mean to me."

I search her eyes, the life we'll build together behind them. "You're not worried this is too fast?"

She bites her bottom lip, shaking her head. "I've been crazy in love since I landed in your arms, babe. And this, what we have, has been the sort of love I've always dreamed of."

I laugh softly, brushing a tear from her cheek as the crowd around us cheers.

"Good," I murmur, pulling her closer.

Because every risk I ever took... every mistake, every broken piece of the past... led me right here.

Right to her.

And loving Izzy?

That's the easiest choice I've ever made.

THE END

A new reggaeton romance set in the Ficha Mundial Universe.

Releasing early 2027.

Follow along for more — and check out the books already out in our shared world.

@fichamundialent

ACKNOWLEDGMENTS

If you're reading this right now, thank you. Seriously. Thank you for spending your time with these characters for a second time.

This book was a long time coming, and I'm so happy and grateful we're finally here—emphasis on the *we*.

I've been incredibly lucky to find such amazing people within this community who constantly support me, inspire me, encourage me, and push me to keep going after this wild dream.

To all the bad ass authors I get to call friends, thank you for inspiring me and reminding me that I really am exactly where I'm meant to be.

To my family, thank you for your patience and for letting my laptop constantly crash our hangouts.

To my Comay, thank you for loving my writing in every form and believing in me even more than I believe in myself sometimes.

To my editors, K.L. and Ken, thank you for your honesty, encouragement, and support. You helped shape this book into something I am extremely proud of.

And finally, thank you to every reader who has supported me, shared these books online, and cared so deeply about these emotionally messy fictional people.

-Kim

ABOUT THE AUTHOR

K. Rodriguez writes sweet and spicy contemporary romance con sazón, centered on real characters, big feelings, and love that hits hard. A first-generation Dominican American author, she loves telling heartfelt stories that feel honest, familiar, and a little messy—in the best way.

Born and raised in Central New Jersey, she traded the northern winters for Southwest Florida, where she lives with her high school sweetheart, their three kids, and four spoiled fur babes.

When she isn't writing, she's homeschooling, wrangling poodles, avoiding the laundry, or blasting her old-school music playlist like it's still 2003.

Stay connected with K. Rodriguez at

www.krodromance.com

Instagram.com/k.rodriguezwrites

Facebook.com/krodwrites